I0632486

Gilbert Parker

When Valmond Came to Pontiac

the story of a lost Napoleon

Gilbert Parker

When Valmond Came to Pontiac
the story of a lost Napoleon

ISBN/EAN: 9783337349943

Printed in Europe, USA, Canada, Australia, Japan

Cover: Foto ©Andreas Hilbeck / pixelio.de

More available books at **www.hansebooks.com**

WHEN VALMOND CAME
TO PONTIAC

THE STORY OF A LOST NAPOLEON

BY

GILBERT PARKER

NEW YORK

STONE & KIMBALL

MDCCCXCVII

TO
MRS. WILSON MARSHALL
VALMOND'S
BEST FRIEND
AND MY
COMRADE
IN HIS
FORTUNES

"Oh, withered is the garland of the war;
The soldier's poll is broken!"

When Valmond Came
To Pontiac

THE STORY OF A LOST NAPOLEON

CHAPTER I

ON one corner stood the house of Monsieur
Garon the avocat; on another, the shop of the Little Chemist ; on another, the office of Medallion
the auctioneer ; and on the last, the Hotel Louis
Quinze. The chief characteristics of Monsieur
Garon's house were its brass door-knobs, and the
verdant luxuriance of the vines that climbed its
sides ; of the Little Chemist's shop, the perfect
whiteness of the building, the rolls of sober wall-
paper, and the bottles of colored water in the
shop windows ; of Medallion's, the stoop that surrounded three sides of the building, and the
notices of sales tacked up, pasted up, on the
front ; of the Hotel Louis Quinze, the deep dormer
windows, its solid timbers, and the veranda that
gave its front distinction—for this veranda had
been the pride of several generations of landlords,

and its heavy carving and bulky grace were worth even more admiration than Pontiac gave to it.

The square which the two roads and the four corners made was, on week-days, the rendezvous of Pontiac, and the whole parish ; on Sunday mornings the rendezvous was shifted to the large church on the hillside, beside which was the house of the Curé, Monsieur Fabre. Travelling towards the south out of the silken haze of a midsummer day, you would come in time to the hills of Maine ; north, to the city of Quebec and the River St. Lawrence ; east, to the ocean ; and west, to the Great Lakes and the land of the English. Over this bright province Britain raised her flag, but only Medallion and a few others loved it for its own sake, or saluted it in the English tongue.

In the drab velvet dust of these four corners, were gathered, one night of July a generation ago, the children of the village and many of their elders.   All the events of that epoch were dated from the evening of this day.   Another day of note the parish cherished, but it was merely a grave fulfilment of the first.

Upon the veranda-stoop of the Louis Quinze stood a man of apparently about twenty-eight years of age. When you came to study him close-ly, some sense of time and experience in his look told you that he might be thirty-eight, though his few gray hairs seemed but to emphasize a certain youthfulness in him.   His eye was full, singularly clear, almost benign ; at one moment it gave the impression of resolution, at another it suggested the wayward abstraction of the dreamer. He was well-figured, with a hand of peculiar whiteness, suggesting in its breadth more the man of action than of meditation. But it was a contradiction, for as you saw it rise and fall, you were struck by its dramatic delicacy ; as it rested on the railing of the veranda, by its latent power. You faced incongruity everywhere. His dress was bizarre, his face almost classical, the brow clear and strong, the profile good to the mouth, where there showed a combination of sensuousness and adventure. Yet in the face there was an elusive sadness, strangely out of keeping with the long linen coat, frilled shirt, the flowered waistcoat, lavender trousers, boots of enamelled leather, and straw hat with white linen streamers. It was a whimsical picture.

At the moment that the Curé and Medallion the auctioneer came down the street together towards the Louis Quinze, talking amiably, this singular gentleman was throwing out hot pennies, with a large spoon, from a tray in his hand, calling on the children to gather them, in French which was not the French of Pontiac—or Quebec ; and this fact the Curé was quick to detect, as Monsieur Garon the avocat, standing on the outskirts of the crowd, had done some moments before. The stranger seemed only conscious of his act of liberality and the children before him. There was a naturalness in his enjoyment which was almost boy-like ; a naïve sort of exultation seemed to possess him.

He laughed softly to see the children toss the pennies from hand to hand, blowing to cool them ; the riotous yet half-timorous scramble for them, and burnt fingers thrust into hot blithe mouths. And when he saw a fat little lad of five crowded out of the way by his elders, he stepped down with a quick word of sympathy, put a half dozen pennies in the child's pocket, snatched him up and kissed him, and then returned to the veranda, where were gathered the landlord, the miller, and Monsieur De la Rivière the young Seigneur. But the most intent spectator of the scene was Parpon the dwarf, who sat grotesquely crouched upon the wide ledge of a window.

Tray after tray of pennies was brought out and emptied, till at last the stranger paused, handed the spoon to the landlord, drew out a fine white handkerchief, dusted his fingers, standing silent for a moment, and smiling upon the crowd.

It was at this point that some young villager called, in profuse compliment, "Three cheers for the Prince!"

The stranger threw an accent of pose into his manner, his eye lighted, his chin came up, he dropped one hand negligently on his hip, and waved the other in acknowledgment. Presently he beckoned, and from the hotel were brought out four great pitchers of wine and a dozen tin cups, and sending the garçon around with one,

the landlord with another, he motioned Parpon
the dwarf to bear a hand. Parpon shot out a
quick, half-resentful look at him, but meeting a
warm, friendly eye, he took the pitcher and went
among the elders, while the stranger himself
courteously drank with the young men of the
village, who, like many wiser folk, thus yielded to
the charm of mystery. To every one he said a
hearty thing, and sometimes touched his greeting
off with a bit of poetry or a rhetorical phrase.
These dramatic extravagances served him well,
for he was among a race of story-tellers and
crude poets.

Parpon, uncouth and furtive, moved through
the crowd, dispensing as much irony as wine :

" Three bucks we come to a pretty inn,
   ' Hostess,' say we, ' have you red wine ? '
          Brave ! Brave !
   ' Hostess,' say we, ' have you red wine ? '
          Bravement !
   Our feet are sore and our crops are dry,
          Bravement ! "

This he hummed to Monsieur Garon the avocat, in a tone all silver, for he had that one gift
of Heaven as recompense for his deformity,—his
long arms, big head, and short stature,—a voice
which gave you a shiver of delight and pain all
at once. It had in it mystery and the incompre-
hensible. This drinking song, lilted just above
his breath, touched some antique memory in the

avocat, and he nodded kindly at the dwarf, though he refused the wine.

"Ah, M'sieu' le Curé," said Parpon, ducking his head to avoid the hand that Medallion would have laid on it, "we're going to be somebody now in Pontiac, bless the Lord! We're simple folk, but we're not neglected. He wears a king's ribbon on his breast, M'sieu' le Curé!"

This was true. Fastened by a gold bar to the stranger's breast was the crimson ribbon of an order.

The Curé smiled at Parpon's words, and looked curiously and gravely at the stranger. Tall Medallion, the auctioneer, took a glass of the wine, and lifting it, said: "Who shall I drink to, Parpon, my dear? What is he?"

"Ten to one, a dauphin or a fool," answered Parpon with a laugh like the note of an organ. "Drink to both, long legs." Then he trotted away to the Little Chemist.

"Hush, my brother," said he, and he drew the other's ear down to his mouth. "Now there'll be plenty of work for you. We're going to be gay in Pontiac. We'll come to you with our spoiled stomachs."

He edged round the circle, and back to where the miller his master, and the young Seigneur stood.

"Make more fine flour, old man," said he to the miller; "pâtés are the thing now." Then, to Monsieur De la Rivière: "There's nothing like hot pennies and wine to make the world love you.

But it's too late, too late for my young Seigneur!"
he added in mockery, and again he began to hum
in a sort of amiable derision:

> " My little tender heart,
>   *O gai, vive le roi!*
> My little tender heart,
>   *O gai, vive le roi!*
> 'Tis for a grand baron,
>   *Vive le roi, la reine;*
> 'Tis for a grand baron,
>   *Vive Napoléon!*"

With the last two lines the words swelled out far
louder than was the dwarf's intention, for few save
Medallion and Monsieur De la Rivière had ever
heard him sing. His concert house was the Rock
of Red Pigeons, his favorite haunt, his other home,
where, it was said, he met the Little Good Folk
of the Scarlet Hills, and had gay hours with them.
And this was a matter of awe to the timid *habitants.*

At the words "*Vive Napoléon!*" a hand touched
him on the shoulder. He turned and saw the
stranger looking at him intently, his eyes alight.

"Sing it," he said softly, yet with an air of command. Parpon hesitated, shrank back.

"Sing it," he persisted, and the request was
taken up by others, till Parpon's face flushed with
a sort of pleasurable defiance. The stranger
stooped and whispered something in his ear.
There was a moment's pause, in which the dwarf

looked into the other's eyes with an intense curiosity, or incredulity—and then Medallion lifted the little man onto the railing of the veranda, and over the heads and into the hearts of the people there passed, in a divine voice, a song known to many, yet coming as a new revelation to them all.

> " My mother promised it,
>   *O gai, vive le roi !*
> My mother promised it,
>   *O gai, vive le roi !*
> To a gentleman of the king,
>   *Vive le roi, la reine ;*
> To a gentleman of the king,
>   *Vive Napoléon !* "

This was chanted lightly, airily, with a sweetness almost absurd, coming as it did from so uncouth a musician. The last verses had a touch of pathos, droll yet searching :

> " Oh, say, where goes your love,
>   *O gai, vive le roi ?*
> Oh, say, where goes your love,
>   *O gai, vive le roi ?*
> He rides on a white horse,
>   *Vive le roi, la reine ;*
> He wears a silver sword,
>   *Vive Napoléon !*
>
> " Oh, grand to the war he goes,
>   *O gai, vive le roi !*
> Oh, grand to the war he goes,
>   *O gai, vive le roi !*

> Gold and silver he will bring,
>   *Vive le roi, la reine ;*
> And eke the daughter of a king—
>   *Vive Napoléon !*"

The crowd, women and men, youths and maidens, enthusiastically repeated again and again the last lines and the refrain, "*Vive le roi, la reine ! Vive Napoléon !*"

Meanwhile the stranger stood, now looking at the singer with eager eyes, now searching the faces of the people, keen to see the effect upon them. His glance found the Curé, the avocat, and the auctioneer, and his eyes steadied successively to Medallion's humorous look, to the Curé's puzzled questioning, to the avocat's birdlike curiosity. It was plain they were not antagonistic (why should they be ?) ; and he—was there any reason why he should care whether or no they were for him or against him ?

True, he had entered the village in the dead of night, with much luggage and many packages, had roused the people at the Louis Quinze, the driver who had brought him departing gayly, before daybreak, because of the gifts of gold given him above his wage. True, this singular gentleman had taken three rooms in the little hotel, had paid the landlord in advance, and had then gone to bed, leaving word that he was not to be waked till three o'clock the next afternoon. True, the landlord could not by any hint or indirection discover from whence this midnight visitor came.

2

But if a gentleman paid his way, and was generous and polite, and minded his own business,
wherefore should people busy themselves about
him? When he appeared on the veranda of
the inn with the hot pennies, not a half dozen
people in the village had known aught of his presence in Pontiac. The children came first to
scorch their fingers and fill their pockets, and
after them the idle young men, and the *habitants*
in general.

The song done, the stranger, having shaken
Parpon by the hand, and again whispered in his
ear, stepped forward. The last light of the setting sun was reflected from the red roof of the
Little Chemist's shop, upon the quaint figure and
eloquent face, which had in it something of the
gentleman, something of the comedian. The alert
Medallion himself did not realize the comedian in
it, till the white hand was waved grandiloquently
over the heads of the crowd. Then something in
the gesture corresponded with something in the
face, and the auctioneer had a nut which he could
not crack for many a day. The voice was musical,—as fine in speaking almost as the dwarf's
in singing,—and the attention of the children was
caught by the warm, vibrating tones. He ad-
dressed himself to them.

"My children," he said, "my name is—Valmond! We have begun well; let us be better
friends. I have come from far off to be one of
you, to stay with you for awhile—who knows how

long—how long?" He placed a finger meditatively on his lips, sending a sort of mystery into
his look and bearing. "You are French, and so
am I. You are playing on the shores of life, and
so am I. You are beginning to think and dream,
and so am I. We are only children till we begin
to make our dreams our life. So I am one with
you, for only now do I step from dream to action.
My children, you shall be my brothers, and together we will sow the seed of action and reap
the grain ; we will make a happy garden of flowers,
and violets shall bloom everywhere out of our
dream,—everywhere. Violets, my children, pluck
the wild violets, and bring them to me, and I will
give you silver for them, and I will love you.
Never forget," he added with a swelling voice,
"that you owe your first duty to your mothers,
and afterward to your country, and to the spirit
of France. I see afar"—he looked toward the setting sun, and stretched out his arm dramatically,
yet such was the impressiveness of his voice and
person that not even the young Seigneur or Medallion smiled,—"I see afar," he repeated, "the glory
of our dreams fulfilled, after toil, and struggle, and
loss ; and I call upon you now to unfurl the white
banner of justice, and liberty, and the restoration !"

The good women who listened guessed little of
what he meant by the fantastic sermon ; but they
wiped their eyes in sympathy, and gathered their
children to them, and said, "Poor gentleman,
poor gentleman !" and took him instantly to their

hearts. The men were mystified, but wine and rhetoric had fired them, and they cheered him —no one knew why. The Curé, as he turned to leave, with Monsieur Garon, shook his head in bewilderment ; but even he did not smile, for the man's eloquence had impressed him. And more than once he looked back at the dispersing crowd and the picturesque figure posing on the veranda. The avocat was thinking deeply, and as in the dusk he left the Curé at his own door, all that he ventured was: "Singular, a most singular person!"

"We shall see, we shall see," said the Curé, abstractedly, and they said good-night. Medallion joined the Little Chemist in his shop door, and watched the *habitants* scatter, till only Parpon and the stranger were left. Presently these two faced each other, and, without a word, passed into the hotel together.

"H'm, h'm," said Medallion into space, drumming the door-jamb with his fingers, " which is it, my Parpon—a dauphin, or a fool ? "

He and the Little Chemist talked long, their eyes upon the window opposite, inside which Monsieur Valmond and the dwarf were talking. Up the dusty street wandered fitfully the refrain :

" To a gentleman of the king,
Vive Napoléon ! "

And once they dimly saw Monsieur Valmond come to the open window and stretch out his hand, as if in greeting to the song and the singer.

CHAPTER II

This all happened on a Tuesday, and on Wednesday, and for several days, Valmond went about making friends. It was easy to do this, for his pockets were always full of pennies and silver pieces, and he gave them liberally to the children and to the poor, though, indeed, there were few suffering poor in Pontiac. All had food enough to keep them from misery, though often it got no further than sour milk and bread, with a dash of sugar in it of Sundays. As for homes, every man and woman had a house of a kind, with its low projecting roof and dormer windows, according to the ability and prosperity of the owner. These houses were whitewashed or painted white, and had double glass in winter, according to the same measure. There was no question of warmth, for in snowtime every house was banked up with earth above the foundations, the cracks and intersections of windows and doors were filled with cloth from the village looms, and wood was for the chopping far and near. Within these air-tight cubes the simple folk baked, and were happy, content if now and then the housewife opened the one pane of glass which hung on a hinge, or the slit in the sash, to let in the cold air. The occasional opening of the outer door to admit some one, as a rule, sufficed, for out rushed the hot blast, and in came the dry frosty air to brace to their tasks the story-teller and singer.

In summer the little fields were broken with wooden ploughs, and there was the limb of a tree for harrow, the sickle and scythe and flail to do their office in due course ; and if the man were well-to-do, he swung the cradle in his rye and wheat, rejoicing in the sweep of the knife and the fulness of the swathe. Then, too, there was the driving of the rivers, when the young men ran the logs from the backwoods to the great mills near and far: red-shirted, sashed, knee-booted, with rings in their ears and wide hats on their heads, and a song in their mouths, breaking a jam, or steering a crib or raft down the rapids. And the *voyageur* also, who brought furs out of the North down the great lakes, came home again to Pontiac, singing in his patois :

" *Nous avons passé le bois,*
Nous somm's à la rive ! "

Or, as he went forth :

" *Le dieu du jour s'avance ;*
Amis, les vents sont doux ;
Bercés par l'espérance,
Partons, embarquons-nous
A-a-a-a-a-a-a ! "

And, as we know, it was summer when Valmond came to Pontiac. The river-drivers were just beginning to return, and by and by the flax *swingeing* would commence in the little secluded valley by the river, and one would see the bright sickle flashing across the gold and green area, and all the pleasant furniture of summer set forth in pride by the Mother of the House whom we call Nature.

Valmond was alive to it all, almost too alive, for at first the flamboyancy of his spirit touched him off with melodrama. Yet, on the whole, he seemed more natural than involved or obscure. His love for children was real, his politeness to women spontaneous. He was seen to carry the load of old Madame Dégardy up the hill, and place it at her own door. He also had offered her a pinch of snuff, which she acknowledged by gravely offering a pinch of her own, from a dirty twist of brown paper.

One day he sprang over a fence, took from the hands of coquettish Élise Malboir an axe, and split the knot which she in vain had tried to break. Not satisfied with this, he piled full of wood the stone oven outside the house, and carried water for her from the spring. This came from natural kindness, for he did not see the tempting look she gave him, nor the invitation in her eye, as he turned to leave her. He merely asked her name. But after he had gone, as though he had forgotten, or remembered, something, he leaped the fence again, came up to her with an air of half-abstraction, half-courtesy, took both her hands in his, and before she could recover herself, kissed her on the cheeks in a paternal sort of way, saying, "Adieu, my child!" and left her.

The act had condescension in it; yet, too, something unconsciously simple and primitive. Parpon the dwarf, who that moment perched himself on the fence, could not decide which Valmond was just then—dauphin, or fool.

Valmond did not see the little man, but swung away down the dusty road, reciting to himself couplets from *Le Vieux Drapeau.*

> "Oh, come my flag, come hope of mine,
>   And thou shalt dry these fruitless tears;"

and apparently without any connection, he passed complacently to an entirely different song:

> "She loved to laugh, she loved to drink,
>   I bought her jewels fine."

Then he added with a suddenness which seemed to astound himself—for afterwards he looked round quickly, as if to see if he had been heard—"Élise Malboir—h'm! a pretty name, Élise; but Malboir—tush! it should be Malbarre; the difference between Lombardy cider and wine of the Empire."

Parpon, left behind, sat on the fence with his legs drawn up to his chin, looking at Élise, till she turned and caught the provoking light of his eye. She flushed, then was cool again, for she was put upon her mettle by the suggestion of his glance.

" Come, lazy-bones," she said, " come fetch me currants from the garden."

" Come, mocking-bird," answered he, " come peck me on the cheek."

She tossed her head, and struck straight home. " It isn't a game of pass it on from gentleman to beetle."

" You think he's a gentleman ? " he asked.

" As sure as I think you're a beetle."

He laughed, took off his cap, and patted himself on the head. " Parpon, Parpon ! " said he, " if Jean Malboir could see you now, he'd put his foot on you and crush you—dirty beetle ! "

At the mention of her father's name a change passed over Élise, for this same Parpon, when all men else were afraid, had saved Jean Malboir's life at a log chute in the hills. When he died, Parpon was nearer to him than the priest, and he loved to hear the dwarf chant his wild rhythms of the Little Good Folk of the Scarlet Hills, more than to listen to holy prayers. Élise, who had a warm, impulsive nature, in keeping with her black eyes and tossing hair, who was all fire, and sun, and heart, and temper, ran over and caught the dwarf round the neck, and kissed him on the cheek, dashing the tears out of her eyes, as she cried :

" I'm a cat, I'm a bad-tempered thing, Parpon ; I hate myself."

He laughed, shook his shaggy head, and pushed her away the length of his long, strong arms. " Bosh ! " said he, " you're a puss and no cat, and I like you better for the claws. If you hate yourself, you'll get a big penance. Hate ·the ugly like Parpon, not the pretty like you. The one's no sin, the other is."

" Who is he, Parpon ? " she asked in a low voice, not looking at him.

She was beside the open door of the oven ; and it would be hard to tell whether her face was suffering from heat or from blushes. However that might chance, her mouth was soft and sweet, and her eyes were still wet.

"Is he like Duclosse the mealman, or José Lajeunesse, or Garotte the limeburner,—and the rest ? " he asked.

"Of course not."

" Is he like the Curé, or Monsieur De la Rivière, or Monsieur Garon, or Monsieur Medallion ? "

" He's different," she said hesitatingly.

" Better or worse ? "

" More—more "— she didn't know what to say —" more interesting."

" Is he like the Judge Honorable that come from Montreal, or the grand Governor, or the General that travel with the Governor ? "

" Yes, but different—more—more like us in some things, like them in others, and more— splendid. He speaks such fine things ! You mind the other night at the Louis Quinze. He is like—"

She paused. "What is he like?" Parpon asked slyly, enjoying her difficulty.

"Ah, I know," she answered; "he is a little like Madame the American, who came two years ago. There is something—something!"

Parpon laughed again. "Like Madame Chalice from New York—fudge!" Yet he eyed her as if he admired her penetration. "How?" he urged.

"I don't know—quite," she answered a little pettishly. "But I used to see Madame go off in the woods, and she would sit hour by hour, and listen to the waterfall, and talk to the birds, and at herself too; and more than once I saw her shut her hands—like that! You remember what tiny hands she had?" (She glanced at her own brown ones unconsciously.) "And she spoke out, her eyes running with tears—and she all in pretty silks, and a color like a rose. She spoke out like this: 'Oh, if I could only do something, something, some big thing! What is all this silly coming and going to me, when I know, I know I might do it, if I had the chance! O Harry, Harry, can't you understand, and help me?'"

"Harry was her husband. Ah, what a fisherman was he!" said Parpon, nodding. "What did she mean by doing 'big things'?"

"How do I know?" asked the girl, fretfully. "But Monsieur Valmond seems to me like her, just the same."

"Monsieur Valmond is a great man," said Parpon, slowly.

"You know," she cried eagerly; "you know! Oh, tell me, what is he? Who is he? Where does he come from? Why is he here? How long will he stay? Tell me, how long will he stay?" She caught flutteringly at Parpon's shoulder.

"You remember what I sang the other night?" he asked.

"Yes, yes," she answered quickly. "Oh, how beautiful it was! Ah, Parpon, why don't you sing for us oftener, and all the world would love you, and——"

"I don't love the world," he retorted gruffly, "and I'll sing for the devil" (she crossed herself) "as soon as for silly gossips in Pontiac."

"Well, well, what had your song to do with him, with Monsieur Valmond?"

"Think hard, my dear," he said, with mystery in his look. "Madame Chalice is coming back to-day; the Manor House is open, and you should see how they fly round up there." He nodded toward the hill beyond.

"Pontiac 'll be a fine place by and by," she replied, for she had village patriotism deep in her veins. Had not her people lived there long before the conquest by the English?

"But tell me, tell me what your song had to do with Monsieur," she urged again. "It's a pretty song, but——"

"Think about it," he answered provokingly. "Adieu, my child," he went on, mockingly, using Valmond's words, and catching both her hands as he had done; then springing upon a bench by the oven, he kissed her on both cheeks. "Adieu, my child," he said again, and jumping down, trotted out into the road. Back to her, from the dust he made as he shuffled away, there came the words :

> " Gold and silver he will bring,
>   *Vive le roi, la reine !*
>   And eke the daughter of a king—
>   *Vive Napoléon !* "

She went about her work, the song in her ears, and the words of the refrain beat in and out, out and in—" *Vive Napoléon !*" Her brow was troubled, and she perched her head on this side and on that, as she tried to guess what the dwarf had meant. At last she sat down on a bench at the door of her home, and the summer afternoon spent its glories on her, for the sunflowers and the hollyhocks were round her, and the warmth gave her face a shining health and joyousness. There she brooded till she heard the voice of her mother calling across the meadow near, and she arose with a sigh, softly repeating Parpon's words, " He is a great man."

In the middle of the night she started up from a sound sleep, and, with a little cry, whispered into the silence, " Napoleon—Napoleon ! "

She was thinking of Valmond. A revelation had come to her out of her dreams. But she laughed at it, and buried her face in her pillow and went to sleep, hoping to dream again.

CHAPTER III

IN less than one week Valmond was as out-
standing from Pontiac as Dalgrothe Mountain,
just beyond it in the south. His liberality, his
jocundity, his occasional abstraction, his meditative pose, were all his own ; his humor that of the
people. He was too quick in repartee and drollery
for a bourgeois, too " near to the bone " in point, for
an aristocrat, with his dual touch of the comedian
and the peasant. Besides, he was mysterious and
picturesque, and this is alluring to women and to
the humble, if not to all the world. It might be
his was the comedian's fascination, but the flashes
of grotesqueness rather pleased the eye, than hurt
the taste of Pontiac.

Only in one quarter was there hesitation, added
to an anxiety almost painful ; for to doubt or distrust Monsieur Valmond would have shocked the
sense of courtesy so dear to Monsieur the Curé,
Monsieur Garon, the Little Chemist, and even
Medallion the auctioneer, who had assimilated
something of the spirit of those old-fashioned
gentlemen into his bluff, odd nature. Monsieur
De la Rivière, the young Seigneur, had to be
reckoned with independently.

It was their custom to meet once a week at the

house of one or another for a causerie, as the avocat called it.   On the Friday evening of this particular week, all were seated in the front garden
of the Curé's house, as Valmond came over the
hill, going toward the Louis Quinze.   His step
was light, his head laid slightly to one side, as if
in pleased and inquiring revery, and, strangely
enough, there was a lifting of one corner of the
mouth, suggesting a gay disdain.   Was it that
disdain which comes from conquest not important
enough to satisfy ambition ?   The social subjuga-
tion of a village—to be conspicuous and attract
the groundlings in this tiny theatre of life !

He appeared not to see the little coterie, but
presently turned, when just opposite the gate,
and, raising his hat, half paused.   Then without
more ado he opened it, and advanced to the
outstretched hand of the Curé, who greeted him
with a courtly affability.   He shook hands with,
and nodded good-humoredly at Medallion and
the Little Chemist, bowed to the avocat, and
touched off his greeting to Monsieur De la Rivière with deliberation, not offering his hand—this
very reserve a sign of equality not lost on the
young Seigneur.   He had not this stranger at any
particular advantage, as he had wished, he knew
scarcely why.   Valmond took the seat offered
him beside the Curé, who remarked presently :

" My dear friend Monsieur Garon was saying
just now that the spirit of France has ever been
the captain of Freedom among the nations."

Valmond glanced quickly from the Curé to the others, a swift, inquisitive look, then settled back in his chair, and turned, bowing, towards Monsieur Garon. The avocat's pale face flushed, his long, thin fingers twined round each other and untwined, and he spoke in a little chirping voice, so quaint as to be almost unreal :

"I was saying that the spirit of France lived always ahead of the time, was ever first to conceive the feeling of the coming century, and by its own struggles and sufferings—sometimes too abrupt and perilous—made easy the way for the rest of the world."

During these words a change passed over Valmond. His restless body became still, his mobile face steady and almost set ; all the life of him seemed to have burnt into his eyes ; but he answered nothing, and the Curé in the pause was constrained to say :

"Our dear Monsieur Garon knows perfectly the history of France, and is devoted to the study of the Napoleonic times and of the Great Revolution—alas for our people and the saints of Holy Church who perished then !"

The avocat lifted a hand in mute disacknowledgment. Again there was a silence, and out of the pause Monsieur De la Rivière's voice was heard :

"Monsieur Valmond, how fares this spirit of France now ?—you come from France, eh ?"

There was a shadow of condescension and ulterior meaning in De la Rivière's voice, for he had caught the tricks of the *poseur* in their singular guest.

Valmond did not stir, but looked steadily at De la Rivière, and said slowly, dramatically, yet with a strange genuineness also :

"The spirit of France, monsieur, the spirit of France, looks not forward only, but backward, for her inspiration. It is as ready for action now as when the old order was dragged from Versailles to Paris, and in Paris to the guillotine ; when France got a principle and waited, waited——"

He did not finish his sentence, but threw back his head with a sort of reflective laugh.

"Waited for what ?" asked the young Seigneur, trying to conquer his dislike.

"For the Man," came the quick reply.

The avocat rubbed his hands in pleasure. He instantly divined one who knew his subject, though he talked thus melodramatically : a thing not uncommon among the *habitants* and the professional story-tellers, but scarcely the way of the coterie.

"Ah, yes, yes," he said, "for—? monsieur, for—?" He paused, as if to give himself the delight of hearing their visitor speak.

"For Napoleon," was the abrupt reply.

"Ah, yes, dear Lord, yes—a Napoleon—of—of the First Empire. France can only cherish an idea when a man is behind it, when a man lives it, embodies it. She must have heroes. She is a poet, a poet—and an actress."

3

"So said the Man, Napoleon," cried Valmond, getting to his feet. " He said that to Barras, to Rémusat, to Josephine, to Lucien, to—to another, when France had for the moment lost both her idea and her man."

The avocat trembled to his feet to meet Valmond, who stood up as he spoke, his face shining with enthusiasm, a hand raised in broad dramatic gesture, a dignity come upon him, in marked contrast to the inconsequent figure which had disported itself through the village during the past week. The avocat had found a man after his own heart. He knew that Valmond understood whereof he spoke. It was as if an artist saw a young genius use a brush on canvas for a moment; a swordsman watch an unknown master of the sword. It was not so much the immediate act, as the divination, the *rapport*, the spirit behind the act, which could only come from the soul of the real thing.

"I thank you, monsieur ; I thank you with all my heart," the avocat said. " It is the true word you have spoken."

Here a lad came running to fetch the Little Chemist, and Medallion and he departed, but not without the auctioneer having pressed Valmond's hand warmly, for he was quick of emotion, and, like the avocat, he recognized, as he thought, the true word behind the dramatic trappings.

Monsieur Garon and Valmond talked on, eager, responsive, Valmond lost in the discussion of Napoleon ; Garon in the man before him. By many pregnant allusions, by a map drawn hastily on the ground here, and an explosion of secret history there, did Valmond win to a sort of worship this fine little Napoleonic scholar, who had devoured every book on his hero which had come in his way since boyhood.   Student as he was, he had met a man whose knowledge of the Napoleonic life was vastly more intricate, searching, and vital than his own.   He, Monsieur Garon, spoke as from a book or out of a library, but this man as from the Invalides, or, since that is anachronistic, from the lonely rock of St. Helena.   A private saying of Napoleon's, a word from his letters and biography, a phrase out of his speeches to his soldiers, sent tears to the avocat's eyes, and for a moment transformed Valmond.

While they talked, the Curé and the young Seigneur listened, and there passed into their minds the same wonder that had perplexed Élise Malboir; so that they were troubled, as was she, each after his own manner and temperament. Their reasoning, their feelings, were different, but they were coming to the point the girl had reached when she cried into the darkness of the night, "Napoleon ! Napoleon ! "

They sat forgetful of the passing of time, the Curé preening with pleasure because of Valmond's remarks upon the Church, when quoting the First Napoleon's praise of religion.

Suddenly a carriage came dashing up the hill with four horses and a postilion.   The avocat was

in the house searching for a book, but De la Rivière, seeing the carriage, got to his feet with instant excitement, and the others turned to look.
As it neared the house, the Curé took off his beretta
and smiled complacently, a little red spot burning
on both cheeks. These deepened as the carriage
stopped, and a lady, a little lady like a golden
flower, with sunny eyes and face—how did she
keep so fresh in their dusty roads ?—stood up impulsively, and before any one could reach the gate
to assist her entered, her blue eyes swimming
with the warmth of a kind heart—or a warm temperament, which may exist without a kind heart.

Was it the heart or the temperament, or both,
that sent her forward with hands outstretched,
saying :

"Ah, my dear, dear Curé, how glad I am to see
you once again ! It has been two years too long,
dear Curé."

She held his hand in both of hers, and looked
up into his eyes with a smile at once childlike and
naïve—and masterful ; for behind the simplicity
and the girlish manner there was a power, a
mind, with which this sweet golden hair and
cheeks like a rose garden had nothing to do.
The Curé, beaming, touched by her warmth, and
by her tiny caressing fingers, stooped and kissed
them like an old courtier. He had come of a
good family in France long ago,—very long ago,
—and even in this French-Canadian village where
he had taught, and served, and lingered forty

years, he had kept some graces of his youth, and
this beautiful woman drew them out. Since he
came to Pontiac he had never kissed a woman's
hand—women had kissed his; and this woman
was a Protestant, like Medallion!   ·

Turning from the Curé, she held out a hand to
the young Seigneur with a little casual air, as if
she had but seen him yesterday, and said : " Monsieur De la Rivière—what, still buried ?—and the
world waiting for the great touch! But we in
Pontiac gain what the world loses."

She turned to the Curé again, placing a hand
upon his arm :

"I could not pass without stepping in upon my
dear old friend, even though soiled and unpre-
sentable. But you forgive that, don't you ? "

"Madame is always welcome, and always—
unspotted of the dusty world," he answered gallantly.

She caught his fingers in hers as might a child,
turned full upon Valmond, and waited. The Curé
instantly presented him to her. She looked at
him brightly, alluringly, apparently so simply ;
yet her first act showed the perception behind that
rosy and golden face, and the demure eyes whose
lids languished now and then—to the unknowing
with an air of coquetry, to the knowing (did any
know her ?) as one would shade one's eyes to see
a landscape clearly, or make out a distant figure.
As Valmond bowed, a thought seemed to fetch
down the pink eyelids, and she stretched out her

hand, which he took and kissed, while she said
in English, though they had been talking in
French :

"A traveller too, like myself, Monsieur Valmond ? · But Pontiac—why Pontiac ?"

Furtive inquiry shot from the eyes of the young
Seigneur, a puzzled glance from the Curé's, as
they watched Valmond ; for they did not know that
he had knowledge of English ; he had not spoken
it to Medallion, who always sent into his talk several English words.

How did this woman divine it ?

A strange look flashed into Valmond's face, but
it was gone on the instant, and he replied quickly :

"Yes, madame, a traveller ; and for Pontiac,
there is as much earth and sky about it as about
Paris, or London, or New York."

"But people count, Monsieur—Valmond."

She hesitated before the name as if trying to remember it, though she recalled it perfectly; it was
her tiny fashion to pique, appear unknowing.

"Truly, Madame Chalice," he answered instantly, for he did not yield to a like temptation ; "but
the few are as important to us as the many sometimes—eh ?"

She almost started at the *eh*, for it broke in
grimly upon the gentlemanly flavor of his speech.

"If my reasons for coming were only as good
as madame's—" he added.

"Who knows ?" she said, with her eye resting
idly on his flowered waistcoat, and dropping to

the incongruous enamelled knee-boots with their red tassels. She turned to the Curé again, but not till Valmond had added :

" Or the same—who knows ? "

Again she looked at him with drooping eyelids, and a slight smile so full of acid possibilities that De la Rivière drew in a sibilant breath of delight. Her movement had been as towards an impertinence ; but as she caught Valmond's eye, something in it so really boy-like, earnest, and free from insolence met hers, that, with a little way she had, she laid back her head slowly, her lips parted anew, in a sweet, ambiguous smile, her glance dwelt on him with a humorous interest, or flash of purpose, and she said softly :

" Nobody knows—eh ? "

She could not resist the delicate malice of the exclamation, she imitated the *gaucherie* so delightfully. Valmond did not fail to see her meaning, but he was too wise to show it.

He hardly knew how it was he had answered her unhesitatingly in English, for it had been his purpose to avoid speaking English in Pontiac.

Presently Madame Chalice caught sight of Monsieur Garon coming from the house. When he saw her he stopped short in delighted surprise. Gathering up her skirts, she ran to him, put both hands on his shoulders, and kissed him on the cheek.

" Monsieur Garon, Monsieur Garon, my good avocat, my Solon, are the coffee, and the history, and the blest Madeira still *chez-toi ?*" she asked gayly.

There was no jealousy in the Curé; he smiled at the scene with great benevolence, for he was as a brother to Monsieur Garon. If he had any good thing, it was his first wish to share it with him, even to taking him miles away to some simple home where a happy thing had come to poor folk—the return of a prodigal son, a daughter's fortunate marriage, or the birth of a child to childless people; and there together they exchanged pinches of snuff over the event, and made compliments from the same mould, nor desired difference of pattern. To the pretty lady's words, Monsieur Garon blushed, and his thin hand fluttered to his lips. As if in sympathy the Curé's fingers trembled to his cassock cord.

"Madame, dear madame "—the Curé approved by a caressing nod—" we are all the same here in our hearts and in our homes, and if anything be good in them it is because you are pleased. You bring sunshine and relish to our lives, dear madame."

The Curé beamed. This was after his own heart, and he had ever said that his dear avocat would have been a brilliant orator, were it not for his retiring spirit. For himself, he was no speaker at all; he could only do his duty and love his people. So he had declared over and over again, and the look in his eyes said the same now.

Madame's eyes were shining with tears. This admiration of her was too real to be doubted.

" And yet, and yet—" she said, with a hand in the Curé's and the avocat's, drawing them near her, "a heretic, my dear friends ! How should I stand in your hearts if I were only of your faith ? Or is it that you yearn over the lost sheep more than over the ninety and nine of the fold ? "

There was a real moisture in her eyes, and in her own heart she wondered, this fresh and venturing spirit, if she cared for them as they seemed to care for her—for she felt she had an inherent strain of the actress temperament, while these honest provincials were wholly real.

But if she made them happy by her gayety, what matter ? And so the tears dried as she flashed a malicious look at the young Seigneur, as though to say : " You had your chance, and you made nothing of it, and these simple gentlemen have done the gracious thing."

Perhaps it was a liberal interpretation of his creed which prompted the Curé to add with a quaint smile :

" 'Thou art not far from the Kingdom,' my daughter."

The avocat, who had no vanity, hastened to add to his former remarks, as if he had been guilty of an oversight :

" Dear madame, you have flattered my poor gleanings in history ; I am happy to tell you that there is here another and a better pilot in that sea.

It is Monsieur Valmond," he added, his voice chirruping in his pleasure. " For Napoleon——"

" Ah, Napoleon, yes, Napoleon ? " she said, turning to Valmond with a look half of interest, half of incredulity.

" —For Napoleon is, through him, a revelation," the avocat went on. " He fills in the vague spaces, clears up mysteries of incident, and gives, instead, mystery of character."

" Indeed," she added, still incredulous, but interested in this bizarre figure who had so worked upon her old friend ; interested because she had a keen scent for mystery, and instinctively felt it here before her. Like De la Rivière, she perceived a strange combination of the gentleman and—something else ; but, unlike him, she saw also a light in the face and eyes that might be genius, poetry, adventure. For the incongruities, what did they matter to her ? She wished to probe life, to live it, to race the whole gamut of inquiry, experience, follies, loves, and sacrifices, to squeeze the orange dry, and then to die while yet young, having gone the full compass, the needle pointing home. She was as broad as sumptuous in her nature ; so what did a *gaucherie* matter, or this dash of the Oriental in a citizen of the Occident ?

" Then we must set the centuries right, and so on—if you will come to see me when I am settled at the Manor," she said to Valmond. He bowed, expressed his pleasure a little oracularly, and was

about to say something else, but she turned deftly
to De la Rivière, with a sweetness which made up
for her previous irony to him, and said :

"You, my excellent Seigneur, will come to
breakfast with me one day ? My husband will
be here soon. When you see our flag flying, you
will find the table always laid for four."

Then to the Curé and the avocat : "You shall
visit me whenever you will, and you are to wait
for nothing, or I shall come to fetch you. I
am so glad to see you. And now, dear Curé,
will you take me to my carriage ? "

A surf of dust rising back of the carriage soon
hid her from view ; but four men, left behind in
the little garden, stood watching, as if they expected to see a vision in rose and gold rise from it ;
and each was smiling unconsciously.

CHAPTER IV

SINCE Friday night the good Curé, in his calm, philosophical way, had brooded much over the talk in the garden upon France, the Revolution, and Napoleon. As a rule, his sermons were commonplace almost to a classical simplicity, but there were times when, moved by some new theme, he talked to the villagers as if they, like himself, were learned and wise.

His thoughts reverted to his old life in France, to the two Napoleons that he had seen, and the time when, at Neuilly, a famous general burst into his father's house, and with streaming tears cried :

"He is dead—he is dead—at St. Helena—Napoleon ! Oh, Napoleon !"

A chapter of Isaiah came to the Curé's mind. He brought out his Bible from the house, and walking up and down read aloud certain passages. They kept ringing in his ears all day :

"*He will surely violently turn and toss thee like a ball into a large country: there shalt thou die, and there the chariots of thy glory shall be the shame of thy lord's house.* . . .

"*And it shall come to pass in that day, that I will call my servant Eliakim son of Hilkiah :*

"*And I will clothe him with thy robe, and*

strengthen him with thy girdle, and I will com-
mit thy government into his hand.   .   .   .

" And I will fasten him as a nail in a sure
place ; and he shall be for a glorious throne to
his father's house.

" And they shall hang upon him all the glory
of his father's house, the offspring and the
issue.   .   .   ."

His face shone with a gentle benignity, as he
quoted these verses in the pulpit on Sunday morning, with a half smile, as of pleased meditation.
He was lost to the people before him, and when
he began to speak, it was as in soliloquy.   He was
talking to a vague audience, into that space where
a man's eyes look when he is searching his own
mind, discovering it to himself.

The instability of earthly power, the putting
down of the great, their exile and chastening, and
their restoration in their own persons, or in the
persons of their descendants—was his subject.   He
brought the application down to their own rude,
simple life, then returned with it to a higher plane.

At last, as if the memories of France " beloved
and incomparable" overcame him, he dwelt upon
the bitter glory of the Revolution.   Then, with a
sudden flush, he spoke of Napoleon.   At that name
the church became still, and the dullest *habitant*
listened intently.   Napoleon was in the air—a
curious sequence to the song that was sung on
the night of Valmond's arrival, when a phrase
was put in the mouths of the parish, which gave

birth to a personal reality. *"Vive Napoléon!"*
had been on every lip this week, and it was an
easy step from a phrase to a man.

The Curé spoke with pensive dignity of Napoleon's past career, his work for France, his too
proud ambition, behind which was his great love
of country, and how, for chastening, God turned
upon him violently and tossed him like a ball into
the wide land of exile, from which he came out no
more.

"But," continued the calm voice, "his spirit,
stripped of the rubbish of this quarrelsome world,
and freed from the spite of foes, comes out from
exile and lives in our France to-day—for she is
still ours, though we find peace, and bread to eat,
under another flag. And in these troubled times,
when France needs a man, even as a barren
woman a child to be the token of her woman-
hood, it may be that one sprung from the loins
of the great Napoleon may again give life to
the principle which some have sought to make
into a legend. Even as the great deliverer came
out of obscure Corsica, so from some outpost
of France, where the old watchwords still are
called, may rise another Napoleon, whose mis-
sion will be civic glory and peace alone, the
champion of the spirit of France, defending it
against the unjust. He shall be fastened as a
nail in a sure place, as a glorious throne to his
father's house."

He leaned over the pulpit, and, pausing, looked

down at his congregation.   Then, all at once, he
was aware that he had created a profound impression.   Just in front of him, his eyes burning with
a strange fire, sat Monsieur Valmond.   Parpon,
beside him, hung over the back of a seat, his long
arms stretched out, his hands applauding in a
soundless way.   Beneath the sword of Louis the
Martyr, the great treasure of the parish, presented
to this church by Marie Antoinette, sat the avocat, his thin fingers pressed to his mouth as if to
stop a sound, bright spots of excitement burning
on his cheeks.   Presently, out of pure spontaneity,
there ran through the church like a soft chorus :

> " Oh, say, where goes your love ?
>   *O gai, vive le roi !*
> He wears a silver sword,
>   *Vive Napoléon !* "

The thing was unprecedented.   Who had started
it ?   Afterwards some said it was Parpon, the now
chosen comrade—or servant—of Valmond, who,
people said, had given himself up to the stranger,
body and soul ; but no one could swear to that.
Shocked, and taken out of his dream, the Curé
raised his hand against the song.   " Hush, hush,
my children," he said.   " Hush, I command you."
It was the sight of the upraised hands, more
than the Curé's voice, which stilled the outburst.
Those same hands had sprinkled the holy water
in the sacrament of baptism, had blessed man and
maid at the altar, had quieted the angry arm

lifted to strike, had anointed the brow of the
dying, and laid a crucifix on breasts which had
ceased to harbor breath, and care, and love, and
all things else.

Silence fell. In another moment the sermon
was finished, but not till his eyes had again met
those of Valmond, and there had passed into his
mind a sudden, startling thought.   Unconsciously
the Curé had declared himself the patron of all
that made Pontiac forever a notable spot in the
eyes of three nations ; and if he repented of it, no
man ever knew.

During mass and the sermon Valmond had sat
very still, once or twice smiling curiously at
thought of how, inactive himself, the gate of destiny was being opened up for him.   Yet he had
not been all inactive. He had paid much attention to his toilet, selecting, with purpose, the white
waistcoat, the long, blue-gray coat cut in a fashion anterior to this time by thirty years or more,
and particularly to the arrangement of his hair.
He resembled Napoleon—not the later Napoleon,
but the Bonaparte who fought at Marengo, lean,
shy, laconic ; and this had startled the Curé in his
pulpit, and the rest of the little coterie.

But Madame Chalice, sitting not far from Élise
Malboir, had seen the resemblance in the Curé's
garden on Friday evening ; and though she had
laughed at it,—for, indeed, the matter was ludi-
crous enough at first,—the impression had remained.

She was no Catholic, she did not as a rule care for religious services, but there was interest in the air, she was restless, the morning was inviting, she was reverent of all true expression of life and feeling, though a sad mocker in much ; and so she had come to the little church.

Following Élise's intent look, she read with amusement the girl's budding romance, and was then suddenly arrested by the head of Valmond, now half turned towards her. It had, indeed, a look of the First Napoleon. Was it the hair ? Yes, it must be ; but the head was not so square, so firm-set, and what a world of difference in the grand effect ! The one had been distant, splendid, brooding (so she glorified him) ; the other was an impressionist imitation, with dash, form, poetry, and color. But the great strength ? It was lacking. The close association of Parpon and Valmond— that was droll ; yet, too, it had a sort of fitness, she knew scarcely why. However, it proved that monsieur was not a fool, in the vulgar sense, for he had made a friend of a little creature who could be a wasp or a humming-bird, as he pleased. Then, too, the stranger had conquered her dear avocat ; had won the hearts of the mothers and daughters— her own servants talked of no one else ; had captured this pretty Élise Malboir ; had made the young men imitate his walk and retail his sayings ; had won from herself an invitation to visit her ; and now, making an unconscious herald and champion of an innocent old Curé, had set a whole

4

congregation singing *"Vive Napoléon"* after mass.

Napoleon? She threw back her pretty head, laughed softly, and fanned herself. Napoleon? Why, of course, there could be no real connection; the man was an impostor, a base impostor, playing upon the credulities of a secluded village. Absurd—and interesting! So interesting, she did not resent the attention given to Valmond, to the exclusion of herself; though, to speak truly, her vanity desired not admiration more than is inherent in the race of women, whose way to power, through centuries, has been personal influence.

Yet she was very dainty this morning, good to look at, and refreshing, with everything in flower-like accord; simple in general effect, though with touches of the dramatic here and there—in the little black patch on the delicate health of her cheek, in the seductive arrangements of her laces. She loved dress, all the vanities, but she had something that rose above them—an imaginative mind, certain of whose faculties had been sharpened to a fine edge of cleverness and wit. For she was but twenty-three, with the logic of a woman of fifty, without its setness and lack of elasticity. She went straight for the hearts of things, while yet glittering upon the surface.

This was why Valmond interested her—not as a man, a physical personality, but as a mystery to be probed, discovered. Sentiment? Coquetry? Not with him. That for less interesting men, she said.

Why should a point or two of dress and manners affect her unpleasantly? She ought to be just, to remember that there was a touch of the fantastic, of the barbaric, in all genius.

Was he a genius? For an instant she almost thought that he was, when she saw the people make way for him to pass out of the church, as though he were a great personage, Parpon trotting behind him. He carried himself with true appreciation of the incident, acknowledging more by look than by sign this courtesy.

"Upon my word," she said, "he has them in his pocket!" Then, unconsciously plagiarizing Parpon: "Prince or barber—a toss-up, indeed!"

Outside, many had gathered round Medallion. The auctioneer, who liked the unique thing and was not without tact, so took on himself the office of inquisitor, even as there rose again little snatches of "*Vive Napoléon*" from the crowd. He approached Valmond, who was moving on towards the Louis Quinze, with just valuation of a time for disappearing.

"We know you, sir," said Medallion, "as Monsieur Valmond, but there are those who think you would let us address you by a name better known—indeed, the name dear to all Frenchmen. If it be so, will you not let us call you Napoleon" (he took off his hat, and Valmond did the same), "and will you tell us what we may do for you?"

Madame Chalice, a little way off, watched Valmond closely. He seemed to hesitate a moment, yet he was not outwardly nervous, and presently answered with an air of *empressement:*

" Monsieur, my friends, I am in the hands of Fate. I am dumb. Fate speaks for me. But we shall know each other better ; and I trust you, who, as Frenchmen, descended from a better day in France, will not betray me. Let us be patient till Destiny strikes the hour."

For the first time to-day he now saw Madame Chalice. She could have done no better thing to serve him, than to hold out her hand, and say in her clear tones, which had, too, a fascinating sort of monotony :

" Monsieur, if you are idle Friday afternoon, per- haps you will bestow on me a half-hour at the Manor ; and I will try to make half mine no bad one."

He was keen enough to feel the delicacy of the point through the deftness of the phrase ; and what he said and what he did now had no pose, but sheer gratitude. With a few gracious words to Medallion she bowed and drove away, leaving Valmond in the midst of an admiring crowd.

He was launched on an adventure as whimsical as tragical, if he was an impostor ; and if he was not, as pathetic as droll. He was scarcely con- scious that Parpon walked beside him, till the dwarf said :

" Hold on, my dauphin, you walk too fast for your poor fool."

CHAPTER V

F ROM this hour Valmond was carried on by a wave of fortune. Before vespers that night, it was common talk that he was a true son of the great Napoleon, born at St. Helena.

Why did he come to Pontiac? He wished to be in retirement till his friends, acting for him in France, gave him the signal, and then with a small army of French Canadians he would cross the sea, and land in France. Thousands would gather round his standard, and so marching on to Paris, the Napoleonic faith would be revived, and he would come into his own. It is possible that these stories might have been traced to Parpon, but he had covered up his trail so well that no one followed him.

On that Sunday evening, young men and old flocked into his room at the Louis Quinze, shook hands with him, addressing him as " Your Excellency " or " Your Highness," and so on. He maintained towards them a mysterious yet kindly reserve, singularly effective. They inspected the martial furnishing of the room : the drum, the pair of rifles, the pistols in the corner, the sabres crossed on the wall, the gold-handled sword that lay upon the table, and the picture of Napoleon on a white horse, against the wall. Tobacco and wine were set upon a side table, and every man as he passed out, took a glass and enough tobacco for his pipe, and said : "Of grace, your health, monseigneur !"

There were those who scoffed, who from sheer habit disbelieved, and nodded knowingly, and whispered in each other's ears ; but these were in the minority ; and all the women and children declared for "The Man of Destiny." And when some foolish body asked him for a lock of his hair, and old Madame Dégardy (Crazy Joan, as she was called) followed, offering him a pinch of snuff, and a lad appeared with a bunch of violets from Madame Chalice, the dissentients were cast in shadow, and had no longer courage to doubt.

Madame Chalice had been merely whimsical in sending these violets, which her gardener had brought her that very morning.

"It will help along the pretty farce," she had said to herself, and then she sat her down to read Napoleon's letters to Josephine, and to wonder that a woman could have been faithless and vile with such a man. Her blood raced indignantly in her veins, as she thought of it. She admired intellect, supremacy, the gifts of temperament, deeds of war and adventure beyond all. As yet her brain was stronger than her feelings ; there had been no breakers of emotion in her life. A wife, she had no child; the mother in her was spent upon her husband, whose devotion, honor, name, and goodness were dear to her. Yet—yet she had a world

of her own, and reading Napoleon's impassioned
letters to his wife, written with how great homage, in the flow of the tide washing to famous
battlefields, an exultation of ambition inspired her,
and the genius of her distinguished ancestors set
her heart beating hard. Presently, her face alive
with feeling, a furnace in her eyes, she repeated
a paragraph from Napoleon's letters to Josephine :
   "*The enemy have lost, my dearest, eighteen
thousand men, prisoners, killed, and wounded.
Wurmzer has nothing left but to throw himself
into Mantua. I hope soon to be in your arms.
I love you to distraction. All is well. Nothing
is wanting to your husband's happiness, save
the love of Josephine.*"
   She sprang to her feet. "And she, wife of a
hero, was in common intrigue with Hippolyte
Charles at the time ! She had a conqueror, a
splendid adventurer, and coming emperor, for a
husband, and she loved him not. I—I could have
knelt to him—worshipped him. I "— With a
little hysterical, disdainful laugh (as of the soul
at itself) she leaned upon the window, looking into
the village below, alternately smiling and frowning
at the thought of this adventurer down at the
Louis Quinze.
   "Yet, who can tell ? Napoleon dressed infa-
mously, too, before he was successful, and Dis-
raeli was half mountebank at the start," she said.
But again she laughed, as at an absurdity.
   During the next few days Valmond was every-

where—kind, liberal, tireless, at times melan-
choly ; "in the distant perspective of the stage,"
as Monsieur De la Rivière remarked mockingly.
But a passing member of the legislature met and
was conquered by Valmond, and carried on to
neighboring parishes the wondrous tale.

He carried it through Ville Bambord, fifty miles
away, and the story of how a Napoleon had come to
Pontiac, reached the ears of old Sergeant Eustache
Lagroin of the Old Guard, who had fought with
the Great Emperor at Waterloo, and in his army
on twenty other battlefields. He had been at
Fontainebleau when Napoleon bade farewell to
the Old Guard, saying : "For twenty years I have
ever found you in the path of honor and glory.
Adieu, my children ; I would I were able to press
you all to my heart—but I will at least press your
eagle. I go to record the great deeds we have
done together."

When the gossip came to Lagroin, as he sat in
his doorway, babbling of Grouchy, and Lannes,
and Davoust, the Little Corporal outflanking them
all in his praise, his dim eyes flared out from the
distant sky of youth and memory, his lips pursed
in anger, and he got to his feet, his stick pounding
angrily on the ground.

"Tut! tut!" said he. "A lie! a pretty lie!
I knew all the Napoleons—Joseph, Lucien, Louis,
Jerome, Caroline, Eliza, Pauline—all! I have seen
them every one. And their children—pah! Who
can deceive me? I will go to Pontiac, I will see

to this tomfoolery.   I'll bring the rascal to the
drumhead.   Does he think there is no one ? Pish !
I will spit him at the first stroke.   Here, here,
Manette," he cried to his grand-daughter, "fetch
out my uniform, give it an airing, and see to the
buttons.   I will show this brag how one of the Old
Guard looked at Saint Jean.   Quick, my sabre
polish ; I'll clean my musket, and to-morrow I will
go to Pontiac.   I'll put the scamp through his
facings—but, yes ! I am eighty-five, but I have an
arm of thirty !"

True to his word, the next morning at daybreak
he started to walk to Pontiac, accompanied for a
mile or so by Manette and a few of the villagers.

"See you, my child," he said, " I will stay with
my niece, Désire Malboir, and her daughter Élise
there in Pontiac.   You shall hear how I fetch that
vagabond to his pôtage !"

Valmond had purchased a tolerable white horse
through Medallion, and after a day's grooming
the beast showed off very well, and he was now
seen riding about the parish, dressed after the
manner of the First Napoleon, with a cocked hat,
and a short sword at his side.   He rode well, and
the silver and pennies he scattered were most
fruitful of effect from the martial elevation.   He
happened to be riding into the village at one end,
as Sergeant Lagroin entered it at the other, each
going toward the Louis Quinze.   Valmond knew
nothing of Sergeant Lagroin, so that what followed was of the inspiration of the moment.   It

sprang from his wit, and from his knowledge of Napoleon and the Napoleonic history, a knowledge which had sent Monsieur Garon into tears of joy, and afterward off to the Manor House and also to the Seigneury, full of praise of him.

Catching sight of the irate sergeant, the significance of the thing flashed to his brain, and, sitting very straight, Valmond rode steadily down towards the old soldier. The sergeant had drawn notice as he came up the street, and people thronged to their doors, and children followed the gray, dust-covered veteran in his last-century uniform. He came as far as the Louis Quinze, and then, looking on up the road, he saw the white horse, the cocked hat, the white waistcoat, and the long gray coat. He brought his stick down smartly on the ground, drew himself up, squared his shoulders, and said : "Courage, Eustache Lagroin. It is not forty Prussians, but one rogue. Crush him ! Down with the pretender !"

So, with a defiant light in his eye, he came on, the old uniform sagging loosely on the shrunken body, which yet was soldier-like from head to foot. Years of camp and discipline, and battle and endurance, were in the whole aspect of the man. He was no more of Pontiac and this simple life than Valmond himself.

So they neared each other, the challenger and the challenged, the champion and the invader; and quickly the village emptied itself out to see.

When Valmond came so close that he could see

every detail of the old man's uniform, he suddenly reined in his horse, drew him back on his haunches with his left hand, and with his right saluted, not the old sergeant, but the coat of the Old Guard, to which his eyes were directed. Mechanically the hand of the sergeant came to his cap, then, with an angry movement, the old man seemed as though he would attack him.

Valmond sat very still, his right hand thrust in his bosom, his forehead bent, his eyes calmly, resolutely, yet distantly, looking at the sergeant, who grew suddenly still also, while the people watched and wondered.

A soft light passed across Valmond's face, relieving its theatrical firmness, and the half-contemptuous curl of his lip. He knew well enough that this event would make or unmake him in Pontiac. He became also aware that a carriage had driven up among the villagers, and had stopped, and though he did not look directly he felt that it was Madame Chalice. This sudden gentleness was not all assumed ; for the ancient uniform of the sergeant touched something within him, the true comedian, or the true Napoleon, and it seemed as if he might get from his horse and take the old soldier in his arms.

He rode forward, and paused again, with not more than fifteen feet between them. The sergeant's brain was going round like a top. It was not he that challenged, after all.

" Soldier of the Old Guard," cried Valmond, in a

clear, ringing voice, "how far is it to Friedland ? "

Like a machine the veteran's hand went again
to his cap, and he answered :

" To Friedland—the width of a ditch."

His voice shook as he said it, and the world to
him was all a muddle ; for this question Napoleon
the Great had asked a private after that battle
on the Alle, when Berningsen, the Russian, threw
away an army to the master strategist.

The private had answered the question in the
words of Sergeant Lagroin. It was a saying long
afterward among the Old Guard, though it may
not be found in the usual histories of that time,
where every battalion, almost every company, had
a watchword, which passed to make room for
others, as victory followed victory.

"Soldier of the Old Guard," said Valmond again,
" how came you by those scars upon your forehead ? "

" I was a drummer at Auerstadt, a corporal at
Austerlitz, a sergeant at Waterloo," rolled back
the reply, in a high, quavering voice, as memories
of great events blew in upon the ancient fires of
his spirit.

" Ah," answered Valmond, nodding eagerly,
"with Davoust at Auerstadt—thirty against sixty
thousand men. At eight o'clock, all fog and mist,
as you marched up the defile toward the Sonnenberg hills, the brave Gudin and his division feeling
their way to Blucher. Comrade, how still you

stepped, your bayonet before you, clearing the mists, your eyes straining, your teeth set, ready to thrust. All at once a quick moving mass sprang out of the haze, and upon you, with hardly a sound of warning; and an army of hussars launched themselves at your bayonets! You bent that wall back like a piece of steel, and broke it. Comrade, that was the beginning, in the mists of morning. Tell me, how fared you in the light of evening, at the end of that bloody day?"

The old soldier was trembling. There was no sign, no movement from the crowd. Across the fields came the sharpening of a scythe and the cry of the grasshoppers, and the sound of a mill-wheel arose near by. In the mill itself, in a high dormer window, sat Parpon and his black cat, looking down upon the scene with a grim smiling.

The old sergeant saw again that mist fronting Sonnenberg rise up and show ten thousand splendid cavalry and fifty thousand infantry, with a king and a prince to lead them down upon those malleable but unmoving squares of French infantry. He saw himself drumming the Prussians back and his Frenchmen on.

"Beautiful God!" he cried proudly, "that was a day! And every man of the Third Corps that time he lift up the lid of hell and drop a Prussian in. I stand beside Davoust once, and *ping* come a bullet, and take off his chapeau. It fell upon my drum. I stoop and pick it up, and hand it to him,

but I keep drumming with one hand all the time.
'Comrade,' say I, ' the army thank you for your
courtesy.'   'Brother,' he say, ' 'twas to your
drum,' and his eye flash out where Gudin carved
his way through those pigs of Prussians.   'I'd
take my head off to keep your saddle filled, comrade,' say I. *Ping!* come a bullet and catch me
in the calf. 'You hold your head too high, brother,' the general say, and he smile.   'I'll hold it
higher, comrade,' answer I, and I snatch at a
soldier. 'Up with me on your shoulder, big comrade,' I say, and he lift me up. I make my sticks
sing on the leather. 'You shall take off your hat
to the Little Corporal to-morrow if you've still
your head, brother,'—he speak like that, and then
he ride away like the devil to Morand's guns.
Ha, ha, ha ! "

The sergeant's face was blazing, but with a
white sort of glare, for he was very pale, and he
seemed unconscious of all save the scene in his
mind's eye. "Ha, ha, ha!" he laughed again.
" Beautiful God, how did Davoust bring us on up
to Sonnenberg !   And next day I saw the Little
Corporal. 'Drummer,' say he, 'no head's too
high for my Guard. Come, you, comrade, your
general gives you to me. Come, Corporal Lagroin,' he call ; and I come. 'But, first,' he say,
' up on the shoulder of your big soldier again,
and play.' 'What shall I play, sire ? ' I ask. 'Play
ten thousand heroes to Walhalla,' he answer.
I play, and I think of my brother Jacques,

who went fighting to heaven the day before. Beautiful God, that was a day at Auerstadt!"

"Soldier," said Valmond, waving his hand, "step on. There is a drum at the Louis Quinze. Let us go together, comrade."

The old sergeant was in a dream. He wheeled, the crowd made way for him, and at the neck of the white horse he came on to the hotel. As they passed the carriage of Madame Chalice, Valmond made no sign. They stopped in front of the hotel, and Valmond, motioning to the garçon, gave him an order. The old sergeant stood silent, his eyes full fixed upon him. In a moment the boy came out with the drum. Valmond took it, and holding it in his hands, said softly:

"Soldier of the Old Guard, here is a drum of France."

Without a word the old man took the drum, his fingers trembling as he fastened it to his belt. When he seized the sticks, all trembling ceased, and his hands and body grew steady. He was living in the past entirely.

"Soldier," said Valmond, in a loud voice, "re-member Austerlitz. The Heights of Pratzen are before you. Play up the feet of the army."

For an instant the old man did not move, and then a sullen sort of look came over his face. He was not a drummer at Austerlitz, and for the in-stant he did not remember the tune the drummers played.

"Soldier," said Valmond, softly, " with 'The

Little Sword that Danced,' play up the feet of the army."

A light broke over the old man's face. The swift look he cast on Valmond had no distrust now. Instantly his hand went to his cap.

"My General!" he said, and stepped in front of the white horse. There was a moment's pause, and then the sergeant's arms were raised, and down came the sticks with a rolling rattle on the leather. They sent a shiver of feeling through the village, and turned the meek white horse into a charger of war. No man laughed at the drama performed in Pontiac that day, not even the little coterie who were present, not even Monsieur De la Rivière, whose brow was black with hatred, for he had watched the eyes of Madame Chalice fill with tears at the old sergeant's tale of Auerstadt, had noticed her admiring glance "at this damned comedian," as he now designated Valmond. When he came to the carriage of Madame Chalice, she said with oblique suggestion:

" What do you think of it? "

" Impostor! Fakir!" was his sulky reply.

" If fakirs and impostors are so convincing, dear monsieur, why be yourself longer? . . . Listen!" she commanded abruptly.

Valmond had spoken down at the aged drummer, whose arms were young again, as once more he marched on Pratzen. Suddenly from the sergeant's lips there broke, in a high shaking voice, to the rattle of the drum:

> " *Conscrits au pas ;*
> *Ne pleurez pas ;*
> *Ne pleurez pas ;*
> *Marchez au pas,*
> *Au pas, au pas, au pas, au pas !* "

They had not gone twenty yards before fifty men and boys, caught in the inflammable moment, sprang out from the crowd, fell involuntarily, into rough marching order, and joined in the inspiring refrain :

> " *Marchez au pas,*
> *Au pas, au pas, au pas, au pas !* "

The old man in front was charged anew. All at once, at a word from Valmond, he broke into the Marseillaise, with his voice and with his drum. To these Frenchmen of an age before the Revolution, the Marseillaise had only been a song. Now in their ignorant breasts there waked the spirit of France, and from their throats there burst out with a half-delirious ecstasy :

> " *Allons, enfants de la patrie,*
> *Le jour de gloire est arrivé.*"

As they neared the Louis Quinze a dozen men, just arrived in the village, returned from river-driving, carried away by the chant, tumultuously joined the cavalcade, and so came on in a fever of vague patriotism. A false note in the proceedings,

5

a mismove on the part of Valmond, would easily have made the thing ridiculous; but even to Madame Chalice, with her keen artistic sense, it had a pathetic sort of dignity, by virtue of its rude earnestness, its raw sincerity. She involuntarily thought of the great Napoleon and his toy kingdom of Elbe, of Garibaldi and his handful of patriots. There were depths here, and she knew it.

"Even the pantaloon may have a soul,—or a king may have a heart," she said.

In front of the Louis Quinze, Valmond waved his hand for a halt, and the ancient drummer wheeled and faced him, fronting the crowd. Valmond was pale, and his eyes burned like restless ghosts. The Cupid bow of the thin Napoleonic lips, the distant yet piercing look of the Great Emperor, manifested itself in this man with startling distinctness as he waved his hand again, and the crowd became silent.

"My children," said he, "we have made a good beginning. Once more among you the antique spirit lives. From you may come the quickening of our beloved country; for she is yours, though here under the flag of our ancient and amiable enemy you wait the hour of your return to her. In you there is nothing mean or dull; you are true Frenchmen. My love is with you. And you and I, true to each other, may come into our own again—over there!"

He pointed to the East.

"Through you and me may France be born again, and in the villages and fields and houses of Normandy and Brittany you may, as did your ancestors, live in peace, and bring your bones to rest in that blessed and honorable ground. My children, my heart is full. Let us move on together. Napoleon from St. Helena calls to you. Napoleon in Pontiac calls to you! Will you come ?"

Reckless cheering followed ; many were carried away into foolish tears, and Valmond sat still and let them kiss his hand, while pitchers of wine went round.

Again he raised his hand, and getting silence with a gesture, he opened his waistcoat, and took from his bosom an order fastened to a little bar of gold.

"Drummer," he said, in a clear full tone, "call the army to attention."

The old man set their blood tingling with the impish sticks.

"I advance Sergeant Lagroin of the Old Guard, of glorious memory, to the rank of Captain in my Household Troops, and I command you to obey him as such."

His look then bent upon the crowd as Napoleon's might have done on the Third Corps.

"Drummer, call the army to attention," fell the words again.

And like a small whirlwind of hailstones the sticks shook on the drum.

"I advance Captain Lagroin to the rank of Colonel in my Household Troops, and I command you to obey him as such."

And once more : "Drummer, call the army to attention."

The sticks rang down, but they faltered a little, for the drummer was trembling now.

"I advance Colonel Lagroin to the rank of General in my Household Troops, and I command you to obey him as such."

He beckoned, and the old man drew near. Stooping, he pinned the order upon his breast. When the sergeant saw what it was, he turned pale, and the drumsticks fell from his shaking hands. His eyes shone like sun on wet glass, then tears sprang from them upon his face. He caught Valmond's hand and kissed it, and cried, oblivious of them all :

"Ah, sire ! sire ! It is true. It is true. I know that ribbon, and I know you are a Napoleon. Sire, I love you, and I will die for you !"

For the first time that day a touch of the fantastic came into Valmond's manner.

"General," said he, "the centuries look down on us as they looked down on him—your sire—and mine !"

He doffed his hat, and the hats of all likewise came off in a strange quiet. A cheer followed, and Valmond motioned for the wine to go round freely. Then he got off his horse, and taking the weeping old man by the arm, himself loosening the drum from his belt, they walked into the hotel.

"A cheerful bit of foolery and treason!" said De la Rivière to Madame Chalice.

"My dear Seigneur, if you only had more humor and less patriotism!" she answered. "Treason may have its virtues. It certainly is interesting, which, in your present gloomy state, you are not."

"I wonder, madame, that you can countenance this imposture," he broke out.

"Excellent and superior monsieur, I wonder sometimes that I can countenance you. Breakfast with me on Sunday, and perhaps I will tell you why—at twelve o'clock."

She drove on, but meeting the Curé, stopped her carriage.

"Why so grave, my dear Curé?" she said, holding out her hand.

He fingered the gold cross upon his breast—she had given it to him two years before.

"I am going to counsel him—Monsieur Valmond," he said. Then, with a sigh: "He sent me two hundred dollars for the altar to-day, and fifty dollars to buy new cassocks for myself."

"Come in the morning and tell me what he says," she answered; "and bring our dear avocat."

As she looked from her window an hour later she saw bonfires burning, and up from the village came the old song that had prefaced a drama in Pontiac.

But Elise Malboir had a keener interest that
night, for Valmond and Parpon brought her uncle,
"General Lagroin," in honor to her mother's cottage ; and she sat listening dreamily as Valmond
and the old man talked of great things to be done.

CHAPTER VI

PRINCE or plebeian, Valmond played his part with equal *aplomb* at the simple home of Elise Malboir, and at the Manor Hilaire where Madame Chalice received him. On this occasion there was nothing bizarre in Valmond's dress. He was in black—long coat, silk stockings, the collar of his waistcoat faced with white, his neckerchief white and full, his enamelled shoes adorned with silver buckles. His present repose and decorum contrasted strangely with the fanciful display at his first introduction. Madame Chalice approved instantly, for though the costume was in itself an affectation, previous to the time by a generation, it was in the picture, was sedately refined. She welcomed him in the salon where many another distinguished man had been entertained, from Frontenac, and Vaudreuil, down to Sir Guy Carleton. The Manor belonged to her husband's people seventy-five years before, and though, as a banker in New York, Monsieur Chalice had become an American of the Americans, at her request he had bought back from a kinsman the old place as it stood, furniture and all. Bringing the antique plate, china, and bric-à-brac, made in France when Henri Quatre was king, she had fared away to Quebec, set the old mansion in order, and was happy for a whole summer, as was her husband, the best of fishermen and sportsmen.

The Manor stood on a knoll, behind which, steppe on steppe, climbed the hills, till they ended in Dalgrothe Mountain. Beyond the mountain were unexplored regions, hill and valley floating into hill and valley, lost in a miasmic haze, ruddy, silent, untenanted, save mayhap by the strange people known as the Little Good Folk of the Scarlet Hills.

The house had been built in the seventeenth century, and the walls were very thick, to keep out both cold and attack. Beneath the high pointed roof were big dormer windows, and huge chimneys flanked each side of the house. The great roof gave a sense of crouching or hovering, for warmth or in menace. As Valmond entered the garden, Madame Chalice was leaning over the lower half of the entrance door, which opened latitudinally, and was hung on large iron hinges of quaint design, made by some seventeenth century forgeron. Behind her deepened hospitably the spacious hall, studded and heavy beamed, with its unpainted pine ceiling toned to a good brown by smoke and time. Caribou and moose antlers hung along the wall, with arquebuses, powderhorns, and big shot bags, swords, and even pieces of armor, such as Cartier brought with him from St. Malo.

Madame Chalice looked out of this ancient avenue, a contrast yet a harmony; for, though her dress was modern, her person had a rare touch of the archaic, and fitted into the picture like a piece of beautiful porcelain, colored long before the art of making fadeless dyes was lost.

There was an amused, meditative smiling at her lips, a kind of wonder, the flush of a new experience. She turned, and, stepping softly into the salon, seated herself near the immense chimney, in a heavily carved chair, her feet lost in the rich furs on the polished floor. A table at her hand, inlaid with antique silver, was dotted with rare old books and miniatures, and behind her ticked an ancient clock in a tall mahogany case.

Valmond came forward, hat in hand, and raised to his lips the fingers she gave him. He did it with the vagueness of one in a dream, she thought, and she neither understood nor relished his uncomplimentary abstraction ; so she straightway determined to give him some troublesome moments.

"I have waited to drink my coffee with you," she said, motioning him to a seat. "And you may smoke a cigarette, if you wish."

Her eyes wandered over his costume with critical satisfaction.

He waved his hand slightly, declining the permission, and looked at her with an intent seriousness which took no account of the immediate charm of her presence.

"I'd like to ask you a question," he said, with-

out preamble. She was amused, interested.
Here was an unusual man, who ignored the con-
ventional preliminary nothings, beating down the
grass before the play, as it were.

" I was never good at catechism," she answered.
" But I will be as hospitable as I can."

"I've felt," he said, "that you can—can see
through things ; that you can balance them, that
you get at all sides, and——"

She had been reading Napoleon's letters this
very afternoon.

"Full squared ? " she interrupted quizzically.

"As the Great Emperor said," he answered.
" A woman sees farther than a man, and if she
has judgment as well, she's the best prophet in
the world."

"It sounds distinctly like a compliment," she
answered. " You are trying to break that
square ! "

She was a little mystified ; he was different from
any man she had ever entertained. She was not
half sure she liked it.   Yet if he were in very truth
a prince—she thought smilingly of his début in
flowered waistcoat, panama hat, and enamelled
boots !—she should take this confidence as a compliment ; if he were a barber, she could not resent
it ; she could not waste wit or time, she could not
even, in extremity, call the servant to show the barber out ; and in any case she was too comfortably
interested to worry herself with speculation.

"I want to ask you," he said earnestly, " what

is the thing most needed to make a great idea succeed."

"I have never had a great idea," she replied.

He looked at her eagerly, with eyes that were almost boy-like.

"How simple, and yet how astute he is!" she thought, remembering the event of yesterday.

"I thought you had, I was sure you had," he said in a troubled sort of way. He did not see that she was eluding him.

"I mean, I never had a fixed and definite idea that I proceeded to apply, as you have done," she explained tentatively. "But—well, I suppose that the first requisite for success is absolute belief in the idea; that it be part of one's life, to suffer for, to fight for, to die for, if need be—though this sounds like a hand-book of moral mottoes, doesn't it?"

"That's it, that's it," he said. "The thing must be in your bones—*hein?*"

"Also, in—your blood—*hein?*" she rejoined slowly and meaningly, looking over the top of her coffee-cup at him. Somehow again the plebeian quality in that *hein* grated on her, and she could not resist the retort.

"What!" said he, confusedly, plunging into another pitfall. She had challenged him, and he knew it.

"Nothing what—ever," she answered with an urbanity that defied the suggestion of malice. Yet, now that she remembered, she had sweetly challenged one of a royal house for the like lapse into the vulgar tongue. A man should not be beheaded because of a *what*. So she continued more gravely : "The idea must be himself, all of him, born with him, the rightful output of his own nature, the thing he must inevitably do, or waste his life."

She looked him honestly in the eyes. She had spoken with the soft malice of truth, the blind tyranny of the just. She had meant to test him here and there by throwing little darts of satire, and yet he made her serious and candid in spite of herself. He did not concern her as a man of personal or social possibilities—merely as an active originality, who was kin to her in some part of her nature. Leaning back languidly, she was eying him closely from under drooping lids, smiling, too, in an unimportant sort of way, as if what she had said was but a trifle.

Consummate liar and comedian, or true man and no pretender, his eyes did not falter. They were absorbed as if in eager study of a theme.

"Yes, yes, that's it ; and if he has it, what next ?" said he, meaningly.

"Well, then, opportunity, joined to coolness, knowledge of men, power of combination, strategy, and "—she paused, and a purely feminine curiosity impelled her to add suggestively—"and a woman."

He nodded. "And a woman," he repeated after her, musingly, and not turning it to account cavalierly, as he might have done. She saw that he was taking himself with a simple seriousness, that appealed to her.

"You may put strategy out of the definition, leaving in the woman," she added ironically.

He felt the point, and her demure dart struck home. But he saw what an ally she might make. Tremendous possibilities moved before him. His heart beat faster than it did yesterday when the old sergeant faced him. Here was beauty—he admired that; power—he wished for that. What might he not accomplish, no matter how wild his adventure, with this wonderful creature as his friend, his ally, his— he paused, remembering this house had a master as well as a mistress.

"We will leave in the woman," he said quietly, yet with a sort of trouble in his face.

"In your idea ?" was the negligent question.

"Yes."

"Where is the woman ?" insinuated the soft, bewildering voice.

"Here," he answered emotionally ; and he believed it was the truth. She stood looking meditatively out of the window, not at him.

"In Pontiac?" she asked presently, turning with a childlike surprise. "Ah ! yes, yes, I know—one of the people ; quite suitable for Pontiac ; but is it wise ? She is pretty—but is it wise ?"

She was adroitly suggesting Élise Malboir, whose little romance she had discovered.

"She is the prettiest and wisest lady I ever knew, or ever hope to know," he said earnestly, laying his hand upon his heart.

" How far will your idea take you ? " she asked evasively, her small fingers tightening a gold hairpin.

"To Paris, to the Tuileries !" he answered, rising to his feet.

" And you start—from Pontiac ? "

" What difference, Pontiac or Cannes, like the great master after Elbe," he said. " The principle is the same."

" The money ? "

" It will come," he answered. " I have friends —and hopes."

She laughed aloud. She was suddenly struck by the grotesqueness of the situation. But she saw how she had hurt him, and she said with instant gravity :

" Of course, with those one may go far. Sit down and tell me all your plans."

He was about to comply, when, glancing out of the window, she saw the old sergeant, now "General" Lagroin, and Parpon hastening up the walk. Parpon ambled comfortably beside the old man, who seemed ten years younger than he had done the day before.

"Your army and cabinet, monseigneur," she said, with a pretty mocking gesture of salutation.

He glanced at her reprovingly. " My general, and my minister; as brave a soldier, and as able a counsellor as ever prince had. Madame," he added, "they only are *farceurs* who do not dare, and have not wisdom. My general has scars from Auerstadt, Austerlitz, and Waterloo ; my minister is feared—in Pontiac. Was he not the trusted friend of the Grand Seigneur, as he was called here, the father of your Monsieur De la Rivière ? Has he yet erred in advising me ? Have we yet failed ? Madame," he added, a little rhetorically, "as we have begun, so will we end, true to our principles, and——"

"And gentlemen of the king," she quoted provokingly, urging him on.

"Pardon, gentlemen of the Empire, madame, as time and our lives will prove. . . . Madame, I thank you for your violets of Sunday last."

She admired the acumen that had seized the perfect opportunity to thank her for the violets, the badge of the Great Emperor.

"My hives shall not be empty of bees—or honey," she said, alluding to the imperial bees, and she touched his arm in a pretty, gracious fashion.

"Madame—ah, madame ! " he replied, and his eyes grew moist.

She bade the servant admit Lagroin and Parpon. They bowed profoundly, first to Valmond, and afterwards to Madame Chalice. She noted the distinction, and it amused her. She read in the old man's eye the soldier's contempt for women, together with his new-born reverence and love

for Valmond.   Lagroin was still dressed in the
uniform of the Old Guard, and wore on his breast
the sacred ribbon which Valmond had given him
the day before.

" Well, General ? " said Valmond.

" Sire," said the old man, " they mock us in the
streets.   Come to the window, sire."

The *sire* fell on the ears of Madame Chalice
like a *mot* in a play ; but Valmond, living up to
his part, was grave and considerate.   He walked
to the window, and the old man said :

"Sire, do you not hear a drum ? "

A faint rat-tat came up the road.   Valmond
bowed.

"Sire," the old man continued, " I would not
act till I had your orders."

" Whence comes the mockery ? "   Valmond
asked quietly.

The other shook his head.   " Sire, I do not know.
But I remember of such a thing happening to the
Emperor.   It was in the garden of the Tuileries,
and twenty-four battalions of the Old Guard filed
past our great chief.   Some fool sent out a gamin
dressed in regimentals in front of one of the
bands, and then——"

" Enough, General," said Valmond, " I understand.   I will go down into the village—eh, monsieur ? " he added, turning to Parpon with im-
pressive consideration.

"Sire, there is one behind these mockers," answered the little man, in a low voice.

Valmond turned toward Madame Chalice.   " I know my enemy, madame," he said.

"Your enemy is not here," she rejoined kindly.

He stooped over her hand and kissed it, and bowed Lagroin and Parpon to the door.

"Madame," he said, "I thank you.   Will you accept a souvenir of him whom we both love, martyr and friend of France?"

He drew from his breast a small painting of Napoleon, on ivory, and handed it to her.

"It was the work of David," he continued. "You will find it well authenticated.   Look upon the back of it."   She looked, and her heart beat a little faster.

"This was done when he was alive?" she said.

"For the King of Rome," he replied.   "Adieu, madame.   Again I thank you, for our cause as for myself."

He turned away.   She let him go as far as the door.

"Wait, wait," she said suddenly, a warm light in her face, for her imagination had been touched, "tell me, tell me the truth.   Who are you?   Are you really a Napoleon?   I can be a good friend, a constant ally, but I charge you, speak the truth to me.   Are you—?"   She stopped abruptly. "No, no ; do not tell me," she added quickly.   "If you are not what you claim, you will be your own executioner.   I will ask for no further proof than did Sergeant Lagroin.   It is in a small way yet,

6

but you are playing a terrible game. Do you
realize what may happen ? "

"In the hour that you ask a last proof I will
give it," he said, almost fiercely. "I go now to
meet an enemy."

"If I should change that enemy into a friend—"
she hinted.

"Then I should have no need of stratagem or
force."

"Force ?" she asked suggestively. The drollery
of it set her smiling.

"In a week I shall have five hundred men."

"Dreamer ! " she thought, and shook her head
dubiously ; but, glancing again at the ivory portrait, her mood changed.

"Au revoir," she said, "come and tell me about
the mockers. Success go with you—sire."

Yet she hardly knew whether she thought him
sire or sinner, gentleman or comedian, as she
watched him go down the hill with Lagroin and
Parpon. But she had the portrait. How did he
get it ? No matter, it was hers now.

Curious to know more of the episode in the village below, she ordered her carriage, and came
driving slowly past the Louis Quinze at an excit-
ing moment. A crowd had gathered, and boys
and even women were laughing and singing in
ridicule snatches of, "*Vive Napoléon !*" For, in
derision of yesterday's event, a small boy, tricked
out with a paper cocked hat and incongruous
regimentals, with a hobby-horse between his legs,

was marching up and down, preceded by another lad, who played a toy drum in mockery of Lagroin. The children had been well rehearsed, for even as Valmond arrived upon the scene, Lagroin and Parpon on either side of him, the mock Valmond was bidding the drummer, "Play up the feet of the army."

The crowd parted on either side, silenced and awed by the look of potential purpose in the face of this yesterday's hero. The old sergeant's glance was full of fury, Parpon's of a devilish sort of glee.

Valmond approached the lads.

"My children," he said kindly, "you have not learned your lesson well enough. You shall be taught." He took the paper caps from their heads. "I will give you better caps than these." He took the hobby-horse, the drum, and the tin swords. "I will give you better things than these." He put the caps on the ground, added the toys to the heap, and Parpon, stooping, lighted the paper. Then scattering money among the crowd, and giving some silver to the lads, Valmond stood looking at the bonfire for a moment, and pointing to it dramatically said :

"My friends, my brothers, Frenchmen, we will light larger fires than these. Your young Seigneur sought to do me honor this afternoon. I thank him, and he shall have proof of my affection in good time. And now our good landlord's wine is free to you, for one goblet each.—My children," he added, turning to the little mockers, "come to

me to-morrow, and I will show you how to be
soldiers. My general shall teach you what to do,
and I will teach you what to say."

Valmond had conquered. Almost instantly
there arose the old admiring cries of, "*Vive Napoléon!*" and he knew that he had regained his
ground. Amid the pleasant tumult the three
entered the hotel together, like people in a
play.

As they were going up the stairs, the dwarf
whispered to the old soldier, who laid his hand
fiercely upon the fine sword at his side, given him
that morning by Valmond. Looking down, Lagroin saw the young Seigneur maliciously laughing at them, as if in delight at the mischief he
had caused.

That night, at nine o'clock, the old sergeant
went to the Seigneury, knocked, and was admitted
to a room where were seated the young Seigneur,
Medallion, and the avocat.

"Well, General," said De la Rivière, rising with
great formality, "what may I do to serve you?
Will you join our party?" He motioned to a chair.

The old man's lips were set and stern, and he
vouchsafed no reply to the hospitable request.

"Monsieur," he said, "to-day you threw dirt at
my great master. He is of royal blood, and he
may not fight you. But I, monsieur, his general,
demand satisfaction—swords or pistols!"

De la Rivière sat down, leaned back in his chair,
and laughed. Without a word the old man stepped

forward and struck him across the mouth with his red cotton handkerchief.

"Then take that, monsieur," said he, "from one who fought for the First Napoleon, and will fight for this Napoleon against the tongue of slander and the acts of fools. I killed two Prussians once for saying that the Great Emperor's shirt stuck out below his waistcoat. You'll find me at the Louis Quinze," he added, before De la Rivière, choking with wrath, could do more than get to his feet ; and, wheeling, he left the room.

The young Seigneur would have followed him, but the avocat laid a restraining hand upon his arm, and Medallion said : "Dear Seigneur, see, you can't fight him. The parish would only laugh."

De la Rivière accepted the advice, and on Sunday, over the coffee, unburdened the tale to Madame Chalice. Contrary to his expectations, she laughed a great deal, then soothed his wounded feelings, and counselled him as Medallion had done. And because Valmond commanded the old sergeant to silence, the matter ended for the moment. But it would have its hour yet, and Valmond knew this as well as the young Seigneur.

CHAPTER VII

IT was no vain boast of Valmond's that he would, or could, have five hundred followers in two weeks. Lagroin and Parpon were busy, each in his own way—Lagroin, open, bluff, imperative; Parpon, silent, acute, shrewd. Two days before the feast of St. John the Baptist, the two made a special tour through the parish for certain recruits. If these could be enlisted, a great many men of this and other parishes would follow. They were Muroc the charcoalman, Duclosse the mealman, Lajeunesse the blacksmith, and Garotte the limeburner, all men of note, after their kind, with influence and individuality.

These four comrades were often to be found together about the noon hour in the shop of José Lajeunesse. They formed the coterie of the humble, even as the Curé's coterie represented the aristocracy of Pontiac—with Medallion as a connecting link.

Lagroin chafed that he must be recruiting sergeant and general also. But it gave him comfort to remember that the Great Emperor had not at times disdained to play the same rôle; that, after Friedland, he himself had been taken into the Old Guard by the Emperor; that Davoust had called him brother; that Ney had eaten supper and slept with him under the same blanket. Parpon would gladly have done this work alone, but he knew that Lagroin in his regimentals would be useful.

Arches and poles were being put up to be decorated against the feast-day, and piles of wood for bonfires were arranged at points on the hills round the village. Cheer and good-will were everywhere, for a fine harvest was in view, and this feast-day always brought gladness and simple revelling. Parish interchanged with parish; but, because it was so remote, Pontiac was its own goal of pleasure, and few fared forth, though others came from Ville Bambord and elsewhere to join the *fête*. As Lagroin and the dwarf approached to the door of the smithy, they heard the loud laugh of Lajeunesse.

"Good!" said Parpon. "Hear how he tears his throat."

"If he has sense I'll make a captain of him," remarked Lagroin, consequentially.

"You shall beat him into a captain on his own anvil," rejoined the little man.

They entered the shop. Lajeunesse was leaning on his bellows, laughing, and holding an iron in the spitting fire; Muroc was seated on the edge of the cooling tub, and Duclosse was resting on a bag of his excellent meal; Garotte was the only missing member of the quartette.

Muroc was a wag, a grim sort of fellow, black from his trade, with big rollicking eyes. At times

he was not easy to please, but if he took a liking he
was for joking at once. He approved of Parpon,
and never lost a chance of sharpening his humor
on the dwarf's impish whetstone of a tongue.

"Lord ! Lord !" he cried, with feigned awe,
getting to his feet at sight of the two. Then he
said to his comrades : "Children, children, off with
your hats. Here is Monsieur Talleyrand, if I'm
not mistaken. Onto your feet, mealman, and dust
your stomach. Lajeunesse, wipe your face with
your leather. Duck your heads, stupids !"

With mock solemnity the three greeted Parpon
and Lagroin. The old sergeant's face flushed, and
his hand dropped to his sword ; but he had promised Parpon to say nothing till he got his cue, and
he would keep his word. So he disposed himself
in an attitude of martial attention. The dwarf
bowed to the others with a face of as great gravity
as the charcoalman's, and waving his hand said :

"Keep your seats, my children, and God be with
you. You are right, smutty-face ; I am Monsieur
Talleyrand, minister of the Crown."

"The devil, you say !" cried the mealman.

"Tut, tut," said Lajeunesse, chaffing, "haven't
you heard the news? The devil is dead !"

Parpon's hand went into his pocket. "My poor
orphan," said he, trotting over and thrusting some
silver into the blacksmith's pocket, "I see he
hasn't left you well off. Accept my humble gift."

"The devil dead !" cried Muroc, with a loud
guffaw ; "then I'll go marry his daughter now."

The dwarf climbed up on a pile of untired
wheels, and, with an elfish grin, began singing.
Instantly the three humorists became silent, and
listened, the blacksmith pumping his bellows
mechanically the while.

" O mealman white, give me your daughter,
    Oh, give her to me, your sweet Suzon !
O mealman dear, you can do no better,
    For I have a château at Malmaison.

" Black charcoalman, you shall not have her,
    She shall not marry you, my Suzon—
A bag of meal and a sack of carbon !
    Non, non, non, non, non, non, non, non !
Go look at your face, my *fanfaron*,
    My daughter and you would be night and day.
    Your face would frighten the crows away.
Non, non, non, non, non, non, non, non,
    You shall not marry her, my Suzon."

A better weapon than his waspish tongue was
Parpon's voice, for it, before all, was persuasive. A
few years before, none of them had ever heard him
sing.   An accident discovered it, and afterwards
he sang for them but little, and never when it
was expected of him.   He might be the minister
of a dauphin, or a fool, but he was now only the
mysterious Parpon who thrilled them.   All the soul
cramped in the small body was showing in his
eyes, as on that day when he had sung at the
Louis Quinze.

A face, unseen by the others, suddenly appeared

at a little door just opposite him. It belonged
to Madelinette, the daughter of Lajeunesse, who
had a voice of merit.   More than once the dwarf
had stopped to hear her singing as he passed the
smithy.   She sang only the old *chansons* and the
lays of the *voyageurs*, with a far greater sweetness and richness, however, than any in the parish ; and the Curé could detect her among all others
at mass.   She had been taught her notes, but that
had only opened up possibilities, and fretted her
till she was unhappy.   What she felt she could
not put into her singing, for the machinery, unknown and tyrannical, was not hers.   Twice before she had heard Parpon sing—at mass when the
miller's wife was buried, and he, forgetting the
world, had poured forth all his beautiful voice ; and
on that notable night on the veranda of the Louis
Quinze.   If he would but teach her those songs
of his, give her that sound of an organ in her
throat !

Parpon guessed what she thought.   Well, he
would see what could be done, if the blacksmith
would join Valmond's standard.

He stopped singing.

"That's as good as dear Caron, the *vivandière*
of the Third Corps.   Blood o' my body, I believe it's
better—almost !" said Lagroin, nodding his head
patronizingly.   "She dragged me from under the
mare of a damned Russian that cut me down,
before he got my bayonet in his liver.   Caron !
Caron ! ah, yes, brave Caron, my dear Caron !"

said the old man, smiling through the golden light that the song had made for him, as he looked behind the curtain of the years.

Parpon's pleasant ridicule was not lost on the charcoalman and the mealman, but neither was the singing wasted, and their faces were touched with admiration, while the blacksmith, with a sigh, turned to his fire and blew the bellows softly.

"Blacksmith," said Parpon, "you have a bird that sings."

"I've no bird that sings like that, though she has pretty notes, my bird." He sighed again. "'Come, blacksmith,' said the Count Lassone, when he came here a-fishing, 'that's a voice for a palace,' said he. 'Take it out of the woods and teach it,' said he, 'and it will have all Paris following it.' That to me, a poor blacksmith, with only my bread and sour milk, and a hundred dollars a year or so, and a sup of brandy when I can get it."

The charcoalman spoke up. "You'll not forget the indulgences folks give you more than the pay for setting the dropped shoe—true gifts of God, bought with good butter and eggs at the holy auction, blacksmith. I gave you two myself. You have your blessings, Lajeunesse."

"So, and no one to use the indulgences but you and Madelinette, giant," said the fat mealman.

"Ay, thank the Lord, we've done well that way," said the blacksmith, drawing himself up, for he loved nothing better than to be called the giant, though he was known to many as *petit enfant*, in irony of his size.

Lagroin was becoming impatient. He could not see the drift of this, and he was about to whisper to Parpon, when the little man sent him a look, commanding silence, and he fretted on dumbly.

"See, my blacksmith," said Parpon, "your bird shall be taught to sing, and to Paris she shall go by and by."

"Such foolery!" said Duclosse.

"What's in your noddle, Parpon?" cried the charcoalman.

The blacksmith looked at Parpon, his face all puzzled eagerness, while another face at the door grew pale with suspense. Parpon quickly turned towards it.

"See here, Madelinette," he said in a low voice. The girl stepped inside, and came to her father. Lajeunesse's arm ran round her shoulder. There was no corner of his heart into which she had not crept.

"Out with it, Parpon," called the blacksmith, hoarsely, for the daughter's voice had followed herself into those farthest corners of his rugged nature.

"I will teach her to sing first ; she shall go to Quebec, and afterwards to Paris, my friend," he answered.

The girl's eyes were dilating with great joy. "Ah, Parpon, good Parpon!" she whispered.

"But Paris! Paris! There's gossip for you,

thick as mortar," cried the charcoalman, and the mealman's fingers beat a jeering tattoo on his stomach.

Parpon waved his hand. " Look to the weevil in your meal, Duclosse ; and you, smutty-face, leave true things to your betters. Mind what I say, blacksmith," he added, "she shall go to Quebec, and after that to Paris." Here he got off the wheels and stepped out into the centre of the shop. " Our master will do that for you. I swear for him, and who can say that Parpon was ever a liar ? "

The blacksmith's hand tightened on his daughter's shoulder. He was trembling with excitement.

"Is it true ? Is it true ? " he asked, and the sweat stood out on his forehead.

" He sends this for Madelinette," answered the dwarf, handing over a little bag of gold to the girl, who drew back. But Parpon went close to her and gently forced it into her hands.

"Open it," he said. She did so, and the blacksmith's eyes gloated on the gold. Muroc and Duclosse drew near, and so they stood for a little while, all looking and exclaiming.

Presently Lajeunesse scratched his head. " Nobody does nothing for nothing," said he. " What horse do I shoe for this ? "

"La, la ! " said the charcoalman, sticking a thumb in the blacksmith's side, "you only give him the happy hand—like that ! "

Duclosse was more serious. " It is the will of God that you become a marshal or a duke," he said wheezingly. "You can't say no; it is the will of God, and you must bear it like a man."

The child saw further; perhaps the artistic strain in her gave her keener reasoning.

"Father," she said, "Monsieur Valmond wants you for a soldier."

"Wants *me?*" he roared in astonishment. "Who's to shoe the horses a week days, and throw the weight o' Sundays after mass? Who's to handle a stick for the Curé when there's fighting among the river-men? But, there, la, la! many a time my wife, my good Florienne, said to me, ' José—José Lajeunesse, with a chest like yours, you ought to be a corporal at least.'"

Parpon beckoned to Lagroin, and nodded.

"Corporal! corporal!" said Lagroin; "in a week you shall be a lieutenant, and a month shall make you a captain, and maybe better than that!"

"Better than that—bagosh!" cried the charcoalman, in surprise, proudly using the innocuous English oath.

"Better than that; sutler, maybe?" said the mealman, smacking his lips.

"Better than that," replied Lagroin, swelling with importance. "Ay, ay, my dears, great things are for you. I command the army, and I have free hand from my master. Ah, what joy to serve a Napoleon once again! What joy! Lord, how I remember——"

"Better than that—eh?" persisted Duclosse,

perspiring, the meal on his face making a sort of paste.

"A general or a governor, my children," said Lagroin. "First in, first served. Best men, best pickings. But every man must love his chief, and serve him with blood and bayonet, and march o' nights if need, and limber up the guns if need, and shoe a horse if need, and draw a cork if need, and cook a potato if need, and be a hussar, or a tirailleur, or a trencher, or a general, if need. But yes, that's it ; no pride but the love of France and the cause, and——"

"And Monsieur Valmond," said the charcoal-man, slyly.

"And Monsieur the Emperor !" cried Lagroin, savagely.

He caught Parpon's eye, and instantly his hand went to his pocket.

"Ah, he is a comrade, that ! Nothing is too good for his friends, for his soldiers. See !" he added more calmly.

He took from his pocket ten gold pieces. "'These are bagatelles,' said his Excellency to me ; 'but tell my friends, Monsieur Muroc, and Monsieur Duclosse, and Monsieur Lajeunesse, and Monsieur Garotte, that they are buttons for the coats of my sergeants, and that my captains' coats have ten times as many buttons. Tell them,' said he, 'that my friends shall share my fortunes ; that France needs us ; that Pontiac shall be called the nest of heroes. Tell them that I will come to them at nine o'clock to-night, and we will swear fidelity.' "

"And a damned good speech too—bagosh !" cried the mealman, his fingers hungering for the gold pieces.

"We're to be captains pretty soon—eh ?" asked Muroc.

"As quick as I've taught you to handle a company," answered Lagroin, with importance.

"I was a patriot in '37," said Muroc. "I went against the English ; I held a bridge for two hours. I have my musket yet."

"I am a patriot now," urged Duclosse. "Why the devil not the English first, then go to France, and lick the Bourbons !"

"They're a skittish lot, the Bourbons ; they might take it in their heads to fight," suggested Muroc, with a grin.

"What the devil do you expect ?" roared the blacksmith, blowing the bellows hard in his excitement, one arm still round his daughter's shoulder. "D'you think we're going to play leap-frog into the Tuileries ? There's blood to let, and we're to let it !"

"Good, my leeches!" cried the dwarf, "you shall have blood to suck. But we'll leave the English be. France first, then our dogs will take a snap at the flag on the citadel yonder." He nodded in the direction of Quebec.

Lagroin then put five gold pieces each in the hands of Muroc and Duclosse, and said :

"I here take you into the service of Prince Valmond Napoleon, and you do hereby swear to serve him loyally, even to the shedding of your blood, for his honor and the honor of France; and you do also vow to require a like loyalty and obedience of all men under your command. Swear."

There was a slight pause, for the old man's voice had the ring of a fatal earnestness. It was no farce, but a real thing.

"Swear," he said again. "Raise your right hand."

"Done!" said Muroc. "To the devil with the charcoal. I'll go wash my face."

"There's my hand on it," added Duclosse; "but that rascal Petrie will get my trade, and I'd rather be strung by the Bourbons than that."

"Till I've no more wind in my bellows," responded Lajeunesse, raising his hand, "if he keeps faith with my Madelinette."

"On the honor of a soldier," said Lagroin, and he crossed himself.

"God save us all!" cried Parpon.

Obeying a motion of the dwarf's hand, Lagroin then drew from his pocket a flask of cognac, with five little tin cups fitting into each other. Handing one to each, he poured them brimming full. Filling his own, he spilled a little in the steely dust of the smithy floor. All did the same, though they knew not why.

"What's that for?" asked the mealman.

"To show the Little Corporal, dear Corporal

7

Violet, and my comrades of the Old Guard, that we don't forget them," cried Lagroin.

He drank slowly, holding his head far back, and as he brought it straight again, he swung on his heel, for two tears were racing down his cheeks.

The mealman wiped his eyes in sympathy ; the charcoalman shook his head at the blacksmith, as though to say, " Poor devil ! " and Parpon straightway filled their glasses again. Madelinette took the flask to the old sergeant. He looked at her kindly, and patted her shoulder. Then he raised his glass.

" Ah, the brave Caron, the dear Lucette Caron ! Ah, the time she dragged me from under the Russian mare ! " he said. He smiled into the distance. " Who can tell ? Perhaps, perhaps— again ! "

Then, all at once, as if conscious of the pitiful humor of his meditations, he came to his feet, straightened his shoulders, and cried :

" To her we love best ! "

The charcoalman drank and smacked his lips. " Yes, yes," he said, looking into the cup admiringly, " like mother's milk that ! White of my eye, but I do love her ! "

The mealman cocked his eye toward the open door. " Élise ! " he said sentimentally, and drank.

The blacksmith kissed his daughter, and his hand rested on her head as he lifted the cup, but he said never a word.

Parpon took one sip, then poured his liquor upon the ground, as though down there was what he loved best ; but his eyes were turned to Dalgrothe Mountain, which he could see through the open door.

" France ! " cried the old soldier stoutly, and tossed off the liquor.

CHAPTER VIII

THAT night Valmond and his three new recruits, to whom Garotte the limeburner had been
added, met in the smithy and swore fealty to the
great cause. Lajeunesse, by virtue of his position
in the parish, and his former military experience,
was made a captain, and the others, sergeants of
companies yet unnamed and unformed. The
limeburner was a dry, thin man, of no particular
stature, who coughed a little between his sentences,
and had a habit, when not talking, of humming to
himself, as if in apology for his silence. This
humming had no sort of tune or purpose, and
was but a vague musical sputtering. He almost
perilled the gravity of the oath they all took to
Valmond, by this idiosyncrasy. His occupation
gave him a lean, arid look ; his hair was crisp and
straight, shooting out at all points, and it flew to
meet his cap as if it were alive. He was a genius
after a fashion, too, and at all the feasts and on
national holidays he invented some new feature
in the entertainments. With an eye for the grotesque, he had formed a company of jovial blades,
called Kalathumpians, after the manner of the
mimes of old times in his beloved Dauphiny.

" All right, all right," he said, when Lagroin,

in the half-lighted blacksmith shop, asked him to swear allegiance and service. "'*Brigadier, vous avez raison,*'" he added, quoting a well-known song. Then he hummed a little and coughed. "We must have a show"—he hummed again— "we must tickle 'em up a bit—ho!—touch 'em where they're silly with a fiddle and fife—raddy dee dee, ra dee, ra dee, ra dee !" Then, to Valmond, "We gave the fools who fought the Little Corporal sour apples in Dauphiny, my dear !"

He followed this extraordinary speech with a plan for making an ingenious *coup* for Valmond, when his Kalathumpians paraded the streets on the evening of St. John's Day.

With hands clasped the new recruits sang :

> "When from the war we come,
>   *Allons gai !*
> Oh, when we ride back home,
> If we be spared that day,
>   *Ma luron lurette,*
> We'll laugh our scars away,
>   *Ma luron luré,*
> We'll lift the latch and stay,
>   *Ma luron luré.*"

The huge frame of the blacksmith, his love for his daughter, his simple faith in this new creed of patriotism, his tenderness of heart, joined to his irascible disposition, spasmodic humor, and strong arm, roused in Valmond an immediate liking, as keen, after its kind, as that he had for the Curé and the avocat. With both of these he had had long talks of late, on everything but purely personal matters. They would have thought it a gross breach of etiquette to question him on that which he avoided. His admiration of them was complete, although he sometimes laughed half sadly, half whimsically, as he thought of their simple faith in him.

At dusk on the eve of St. John the Baptist's Day, after a long conference with Lagroin and Parpon, Valmond went through the village, and came to the smithy to talk with Lajeunesse. Those who recognized him in passing took off their *bonnets rouges*, some saying," Good night, your Highness," some, " How are you, monseigneur ?" some, " God bless your Excellency," and a batch of bacchanalian river-men, who had been drinking, called him "General," and insisted on embracing him, offering him cognac from their tin flasks.

The appearance among them of old Madame Dégardy shifted the good-natured attack. For many a year, winter and summer, she had come and gone in the parish, all rags and tatters, wearing men's knee-boots and cap, her gray hair hanging down in straggling curls, her lower lip thrust out fiercely, her quick eyes wandering to and fro, and her sharp tongue, like Parpon's, clearing a path before her whichever way she turned. On her arm she carried a little basket of cakes and confitures, and these she dreamed she sold, for they were few who bought of Crazy Joan.

The stout stick she carried was as compelling as her tongue, so that when the river-men surrounded her in amicable derision, it was used freely, and with a heart all kindness—" for the good of their souls," she said, "since the Curé was too mild, Mary in heaven bless him high and low ! "

For Madame Dégardy was the Curé's champion everywhere, and he in turn was tender toward the homeless body, whose history even to him was obscure, save in the few particulars that he had given to Valmond the last time they had met.

In her youth Madame Dégardy was pretty and much admired. Her lover had deserted her, and in a fit of mad indignation and despair, she had fled from the village, and vanished no one knew whither, though it had been declared by a wandering hunter that she had been seen in the far-off hills that march into the south, and that she lived there with an uncouth mountaineer, who had himself long been an outlaw from his kind. But this had been mere gossip, and after twenty-five years she came back to Pontiac, a half-mad creature, and took up the thread of her life alone ; and Parpon and the Curé saw that she suffered for nothing in the hard winters.

Valmond left the river-men to the tyranny of her tongue and stick, and came on to where the red light of the forge showed through the smithy window. As he neared the door, he heard singing. The voice was singularly sweet, and another of commoner calibre was joining in the refrain :

" ' Oh, traveller, see where the red sparks rise.
          (Fly away, my heart, fly away !)
   But dark is the mist in the traveller's eyes.
          (Fly away, my heart, fly away !)
   ' Oh, traveller, see, far down the gorge,
   The crimson light from my father's forge.
          (Fly away, my heart, fly away !)

" ' Oh, traveller, see you thy true love's grace.'
          (Fly away, my heart, fly away !)
   And now there is joy in the traveller's face.
          (Fly away, my heart, fly away !)
   Oh, wild does he ride through the rain and mire,
   To greet his love by the smithy fire !
          (Fly away, my heart, fly away !) "

In accompaniment some one was beating softly
on the anvil, and the bellows were blowing rhyth-
mically. He lingered for a moment, loath to in-
terrupt the song, and then softly opened the upper
half of the door, for it was divided horizontally,
and leaned over the lower part.

Beside the bellows, her sleeves rolled up, her
glowing face cowled in her black hair, beautiful and strong, stood Élise Malboir, pushing a
rod of steel into the sputtering coals. Over the
anvil, with a small bar caught in a pair of tongs,
hovered Madelinette, beating, almost tenderly, the
red-hot point of the steel. The sound of the
iron hammer on the malleable metal was as muf-
fled silver, and the sparks flew out like jocund
fire-flies. She was making two hooks for her

kitchen wall, for she was clever at the forge, and
could shoe a horse if she were let to do so. She
was but half-turned to Valmond, but he caught the
pure outlines of her face and neck, her extreme
delicacy of expression, which had a subtle, pathetic
refinement, in acute contrast to the quick, abundant health, the warm energy, the half-defiant
look of Élise.   It was an inspiring picture of labor
and life.

A dozen thoughts ran through Valmond's mind.
He was responsible, to an extent, for the happiness of these two young creatures. He had promised to make a songstress of the one, to send her
to Paris, had roused in her wild, ambitious hopes
of fame and fortune—dreams that, in any case,
could be little like the real thing : fanciful visions
of conquest and golden living, where never the
breath of her hawthorn and wild violets entered ;
only sick perfumes as from an odalisque's fan, amid
the enervating splendor of indulgent boudoirs—
for she had read of these things.

In a vague, graceless sort of way, he had
worked upon the quick emotions of Élise. Every
little touch of courtesy had been returned to him
in half-shy, half-ardent glances ; in flushes which
the kiss he had given her the first day of their
meeting had made the signs of an intermittent
fever ; in modest yet alluring waylayings ; in restless nights, in half-tuneful, half-silent days ; in a
sweet sort of petulance. She had kept in mind
everything he had said to her, the playfully emo-

tional pressure of her hand, his eloquent talks with
her uncle, the old sergeant's rhapsodies about him;
and there was no place in the room where he had
sat or stood, which she had not made sacred—
she the madcap, who had lovers by the dozen.
Importuned by the Curé and her mother to
marry, she had threatened, if they worried her
further, to wed fat Duclosse, the mealman, who
had courted her in a ponderous way for at least
three years.

The fire that corrodes, when it does not make
glorious without and within, was in her veins, and
when Valmond should call she was ready to come.
She could not see that if he were in truth a
Napoleon, she was not for him. Seized of that
wilful, daring spirit, called Love, her sight was
bounded by the little field wherein she strayed.

Her arm paused upon the lever of the bellows,
as she saw Valmond watching them from the
door. He took off his hat to them, as Madelinette
turned and said impulsively, "Ah, monseigneur!"
then waited, confused. Élise did not move, but
stood looking at him, her eyes all flame, her
cheeks going a little pale, and flushing again.
She pushed her hair back with a quick motion,
and as he stepped inside and closed the door behind him, she blew the bellows as if to give a
brighter light to the place. The fire flared up,
but there were corners in deep shadow. Valmond doffed his hat again and said ceremoniously,
" Mademoiselle Lajeunesse, Mademoiselle Élise,

pray do not stop your work. Let me sit here and watch you."

Taking from his pocket a cigarette, he came over to the forge, and was about to light it with the red steel from the fire, when Élise, snatching up a tiny piece of wood, thrust it in the coals, and drawing it out held it toward the cigarette, saying : " Ah, no, your Excellency—this ! "

As Valmond reached to take it from her, he heard a sound as of a hoarse breathing, coming from the shadowy corner behind him, and turned quickly ; his outstretched hand touched Élise's fingers, and closed on them involuntarily, all her impulsive temperament and ardent life thrilling through him. The shock of feeling brought his eyes to hers with a sudden burning mastery. For an instant their looks fused and were lost in a passionate affiance. Then, as if pulling himself out of a dream, he released her fingers with a, " Pardon—my child."

As he did so, a cry ran through the smithy. Madelinette was standing, tense and set with terror, her eyes riveted on something that crouched beside a pile of cartwheels a few feet away ; something with shaggy head, flaring eyes, and a devilish face. The thing raised itself and sprang towards her with a devouring cry. Leaping forward with desperate swiftness, Valmond caught the half man, half beast—it seemed that—by the throat ; and Madelinette fell fainting against the anvil.

Valmond was in the grasp of a giant, and,

struggle as he might, he could not withstand the powerful arms of his assailant. They came to their knees on the ground, where they clutched and strained for a wild minute, Valmond desperately fighting to keep the huge bony fingers from his neck. Suddenly the creature's knee touched the red-hot steel that Madelinette had dropped, and with a snarl he flung Valmond back against the anvil, his head striking the iron with a sickening thud. Then, seizing the steel, he raised it to plunge the still glowing point into his victim's eyes.

Centuries of doom seemed crowded into that instant of time. Valmond caught the giant's wrist with both hands, and with a mighty effort wrenched himself aside. His heart seemed to strain and burst, and just as he felt the end was come, he heard something crash on the murderer's skull, and the great creature fell with a gurgling sound, and lay like a parcel of loose bones across his knees. Valmond raised himself, a strange, dull wonder on him, for as the weapon smote this lifeless thing, he had seen another hurl by and strike the opposite wall. A moment afterwards the dead man was pulled away by Parpon. Trying to rise, he felt blood trickling down his neck, and he turned sick and blind. As the world slipped away from him, a soft shoulder caught his head, and out of a great distance there came to him a woman's wailing cry: "He is dying! my love! my love!"

Peril and pain had brought to Élise's breast

the one being in the world for her, the face that had burned like a picture upon her eyes and heart.

Parpon groaned with a strange horror as he dragged the body from Valmond. For a moment he knelt gasping beside the uncouth form, his great hands spasmodically feeling the pulseless breast.

Soon afterwards in the blacksmith's house the two girls huddled together in each other's arms, and Valmond, shaken and weak, returned to the smithy.

In the dull glare of the forge fire knelt Parpon, rocking back and forth beside the body. Hearing him approach, the dwarf got to his feet.

" You have killed him," he said, pointing.

" No, no, not I," answered Valmond. "Some-one threw a hammer."

" There were two hammers."

" It was Élise ? " asked Valmond, with a shud-der.

" No, not Élise ; it was you," said the dwarf, with a strange insistence.

" I tell you no," said Valmond. " It was you, Parpon."

" By God ! it is a lie ! " cried the dwarf, with a groan. Then he came close to Valmond. " He was—my brother ! Do you not see ? " he de-manded fiercely, his eyes full of misery. " Do you not see, that it was you who killed him ? Yes, yes, it was you."

Stooping, Valmond caught the little man in an

embrace. "It was I that killed him, Parpon. It was I, comrade. You saved my life," he added significantly.

"The girl threw, but missed," said the dwarf. "She does not know but that she struck him."

"She must be told."

"I will tell her that you killed him. Leave it to me—all to me, my grand seigneur!"

A half hour afterwards the avocat, the Curé, the Little Chemist, had heard the story as the dwarf told it, and Valmond returned to the Louis Quinze a hero. For hours the *habitants* gathered under his window and cheered him.

Parpon sat long in gloomy silence by his side, but at last, raising his voice, he began to sing softly a lament for the lifeless body, lying alone in a shed near the deserted smithy.

" Children, the house is empty,
   The house behind the tall hill ;
   Lonely and still is the empty house.
   There is no face in the doorway,
   There is no fire in the chimney.
   Come and gather beside the gate,
   Little Good Folk of the Scarlet Hills.
   Where has the wild dog vanished ?
   Where has the swift foot gone ?
   Where is the hand that found the good fruit,
   That made a garret of wholesome herbs ?
   Where is the voice that awoke the morn,
   The tongue that defied the terrible beasts ?
   Come and listen beside the door,
   Little Good Folk of the Scarlet Hills."

The pathos of the chant almost made his listener shrink, so immediate and searching was it. When the lament ceased there was a long silence, broken by Valmond.

"He was your brother, Parpon—how ?   Tell me about it."

The dwarf's eyes looked into the distance.

"It was in the far-off country," he said, "in the hills where the Little Good Folk come.   My mother married an outlaw.   Ah, he was cruel, and an animal !   My brother Gabriel was born —a giant, with brain all fumbling and wild. Then I was born, so small, a head as a tub, and long arms like a gorilla.   We burrowed in the hills, Gabriel and I.   Then one day my mother, because my father struck her, went mad, left us, and came to—" He paused abruptly.   "Then Gabriel struck the man, and he died, and we buried him, and my brother also left me, and I was alone. Bye and bye I travelled to Pontiac.   Once Gabriel came down from the hills, and Lajeunesse burnt him with a hot iron, for cutting his bellows in the night, to make himself a bed inside them.   To-day he came again to do some terrible thing to the blacksmith or the girl, and you have seen—ah, the poor Gabriel, and I killed him ! "

"I killed him," said Valmond, "I, Parpon, my friend."

"My poor fool, my wild dog," wailed the dwarf, mournfully.

;" Parpon," asked Valmond, suddenly, "where is your mother ?"

"It is no matter. She has forgotten—she is safe."

"If she should see him !" said Valmond, tentatively, for a sudden thought had come to him that the mother of these misfits of God was Madame Dégardy.

Parpon sprang to his feet. " She shall not see him. Ah, you know ! You have guessed ?" he cried.

"She is all safe with me."

"She shall not see him. She shall not know," repeated the dwarf, his eyes huddling back in his head with anguish.

"Does she not remember you ?"

"She does not remember the living, but she would remember the dead. She shall not know," he cried again.

Then seizing Valmond's hand, he kissed it, and, without a word, trotted from the room, a ludicrously pathetic figure.

CHAPTER IX

Now and again the moon showed through the cloudy night, and the air was soft and kind. Parpon left behind him the village street, and after a half mile or more of travel came to a spot where a crimson light showed beyond a little hill. He halted a moment, as if to think and listen, then crawled swiftly up the bank and looked down. Beside a still smoking lime-kiln, an abandoned fire was burning down into red coals. The little hut of the limeburner was beyond in a hollow, and behind that again was a lean-to, like a small shed or stable. Hither stole the dwarf, pausing on his way to listen a moment at the door of the hut.

Leaning into the darkness of the shed he gave a soft crooning call. A low growl came in quick reply, followed by others. He stepped inside.

"Good dogs, good dogs, good Musket, Coffee, Filthy, Jo-Jo—steady, steady, idiots!" for the huge brutes were nosing him, throwing themselves against him, and whining gratefully. Feeling against the wall he took down some harness, and in the dark put a set on each dog—mere straps for the shoulders, halters and traces; called to them sharply to be quiet, and, keeping hold of their col-

8

lars, led them out into the night. He paused to listen again. Presently he drove the dogs across the road, and attached them to a flat vehicle without wheels or runners, used by Garotte for the drawing of lime and stones. It was not so heavy as many machines of the kind, and at a quick word from the dwarf, the dogs darted away. Unseen, a mysterious figure hurried on after them, keeping well in the shadow of the trees fringing the side of the road.

Parpon drove the dogs down a lonely side lane to the village, and came to the shed where lay the uncouth thing, which he had called his brother. He felt for a spot where there was a loose board, forced it and another with his strong fingers, and crawled in. Reappearing, with the body, he bore it in his huge arms to the stone-boat: a midget carrying a giant—a dreadful burden. He covered up the face, and returning to the shed, placed his coat against the boards to deaden the sound, and hammered them tight again with a stone, after having straightened the grass about. He found the dogs cowering with a nameless fear, for one of them had pushed the cloth off the dead man's face with his nose. They crouched together, whining and tugging at the traces. With a quieting word he started them away.

The pursuing watchful figure followed at a distance, on up the road, on over the little hills, on into the high hills, the dogs carrying along swiftly the grisly load. And once their driver halted them, and sat in the gray gloom and dust beside the dead man.

"Where do you go, dwarf?" he said aloud.

"I go to the Ancient House," he made answer to himself.

"What do you go to get?"

"I do not go to get, I go to give."

"What do you go to give?"

"I go to leave an empty basket at the door, and the lantern that the Shopkeeper set in the hand of the pedler."

"Who is the pedler, hunchback?"

"The pedler is he that carries the pack on his back."

"What carries he in the pack?"

"He carries what the Shopkeeper gave him— for he had no money and no choice."

"Who is the Shopkeeper, dwarf?"

"The Shopkeeper—the Shopkeeper is the father of dwarfs, and angels, and children,—and fools."

"What does he sell, poor man?"

"He sells harness for men and cattle, and you give your lives for the harness."

"What is this you carry, dwarf?"

"I carry home the harness of a soul."

"Is it worth carrying home?"

"The eyes grow sick at sight of the old harness in the way."

And the watching figure heard and pitied. It was Valmond. Excited by Parpon's last words at the hotel, he had followed, and though suffer-

ing from the wound in his head, and shaken by
the awful accident of the evening, he was keen to
chase this weird adventure to the end.   For, as he
said to himself, some things were to be seen but
once in the great game, and it was worth while
seeing them, even if life were the shorter for it.

On, and ever upward, filed the strange procession, until at last they came to Dalgrothe Mountain.   On one of its foot-hills stood the Rock of
Red Pigeons.   This was the dwarf's secret resort,
and no one ever disturbed him, for it was said the
Little Good Folk of the Scarlet Hills (of whom,
it was rumored, he had come) held revel there,
and people did not venture rashly.   The land
about it, and a hut farther down the hill, belonged
to him, a legacy from the father of the young
Seigneur.

It was all hills, gorges, and rivers, and idle
murmuring pines.   Of a morning, mist floated
into mist as far as eye could see, blue and gray and
amethyst, a glamour of tints and velvety radiance.
The great hills waved into each other like a vast
violet sea, and, in turn, the tiny earth-waves on
each separate hill swelled into the larger harmony.   At the foot of a steep precipice was the
whirlpool from which Parpon had saved the father
of De la Rivière from an awful death, and had
received this lonely region as his reward.   To
the dwarf it was his other world, his real world ;
for here he lived his own life, and it was here he
had brought his ungainly dead, to give it housing.

The dogs drew up the grim cargo to a plateau near the Rock of Red Pigeons, and gathering sticks, Parpon lit a sweet-smelling fire of cedar. Then he went to the hut, and came back with a spade and shovel.   At the foot of a great pine he began to dig.   As the work went on he broke into a sort of dirge, painfully sweet.   Leaning against a rock not far away, Valmond watched the tiny man with the great arms throw up the soft, good-smelling earth, enriched by centuries of dead leaves and flowers.   The trees waved, and bent, and murmured as though they gossiped with each other over this odd grave-digger.   The light of the fire showed across the gorge, touching off the far wall of pines with burnished crimson, and huge flickering shadows looked like elusive spirits, attendant on the lonely obsequies.   Now and then a bird, aroused by the light or the snapping of a burning stick, rose from its nest and flew away ; and wild fowl flitted darkly down the pass, like the souls of heroes faring to Walhalla.   When an owl hooted, a wolf howled far off, or a loon cried from the water below, the solemn fantasy took on the aspect of the unreal.

Valmond watched like one in a dream, and once or twice he turned faint and drew his cloak about him, as if he were cold, for a sickly air, passing by, seemed to fill his lungs with poison.

At last the grave was dug, and sprinkling its depth with leaves and soft branches of spruce, the dwarf drew the body over, and lowered it

slowly and awkwardly. Then he covered all but
the huge, unsightly face, and kneeling, peered
down at it pitifully.

"Gabriel, Gabriel," he cried, "surely thy soul
is better without its harness. I killed thee, and
thou didst kill, and those we love die by our own
hands. But, no, I lie; I did not love thee, thou
wert so ugly, and wild, and cruel. Poor boy!
Thou wast a fool, and—hush! thou wast a murderer. Thou wouldst have slain my prince, and
so I slew thee—I slew thee!"

He rocked to and fro in abject sorrow: "Hast
thou no one in all the world to mourn thee save
him who killed thee? Is there no one to wish thee
speed to the Ancient House? Art thou tossed
away like an old shoe, and no one to say, The
Shoemaker that made thee must see to it if thou
wast illshapen, and walked crookedly, and did evil
things? Ah! is there no one to mourn thee, save
him that killed thee?"

He leaned back, crying out into the great hills
like a remorseful, tortured soul.

Valmond, no longer able to watch his grief in
silence, stepped quickly forward. The dogs, seeing him, growled warningly, and the dwarf looked
up as he heard the footsteps.

"There is another to mourn him, Parpon,"
said Valmond.

A look of bewilderment and joy came into
Parpon's eyes. Then he gave a laugh of singular
wildness, his face twitched, tears rushed down his

cheeks, and he threw himself at Valmond's feet and clasped his knees, crying :

" Ah, ah, my prince, great brother, thou hast come also !   Ah, thou didst know the way up the long hill !   Thou hast come to the burial of a fool. But he had a mother—ay, ay, a mother ! All fools have mothers, and they should be buried well. Ah, come, come, and speak softly the Act of Contrition, and I will cover him up."

He went to throw in the earth, but Valmond pushed him aside gently.

" No, no," he said, " this is for me."   And he began filling the grave.

When they left the place of burial the fire was burning low, for they had talked long.   At the foot of the hills they looked back.   Day was beginning to break over Dalgrothe Mountain.

CHAPTER X

W HEN, next day, in the bright sunlight, the
Little Chemist, the Curé, and others, opened the
door of the shed, taking off their hats in the presence of the Master Workman, they saw that his
seat was empty. The dead Caliban was gone—
who should say how or where? The lock was
still on the doors, the walls were intact, there was
no window for entrance or escape. He had vanished as weirdly as he came.

All day the people sought the place, viewing
with awe and superstition the place where the
body had lain, and the spot in the smithy where,
it was said, Valmond had killed the giant.

The next day was the feast of St. John the Baptist. Mass was said in the church, all the parish
attending ; and Valmond was present, with Lagroin in full regimentals.

Plates of blessed bread were passed round at
the close of the mass, as was the custom on this
feast-day ; and with a curious feeling that came to
him often afterward, Valmond listened to his general saying solemnly :

> " Holy bread, I take thee ;
> If I die suddenly,
> Serve me as a sacrament."

With many eyes watching him curiously, he also ate the bread, and repeated the mystical words.

All day long there were sports and processions, the *habitants* gay in rosettes and ribbons, flowers and maple-leaves, as they idled or filed along the streets, under arches of evergreens, where the tricolor and union jack, amiably mingled and fluttered together. Anvils, with powder placed between, were touched off with a bar of red-hot iron, making a vast noise, and drawing crowds in front of the smithy. On the hill beside the Curé's house was a little old cannon brought from the battlefield of Ticonderoga, and its boisterous salutations were replied to from the Seigneury, by a still more ancient piece of ordnance. Sixty of Valmond's recruits, under Lajeunesse the blacksmith, marched up and down the streets firing salutes with happy intrepidity, and setting themselves off before the crowds with a good many airs, and nods, and simple vanities.

In the early evening, the good Curé blessed and lighted the great bonfire before the church, and immediately, at this signal, an answering fire sprang up on a hill at the other side of the village. Then fire on fire rose up at all points, and multiplied, till all of Pontiac was in a glow. This was a custom set in memory of the old days when fires flashed intelligence, after a set code, across the great rivers and lakes, and from hill to hill.

Far up against Dalgrothe Mountain appeared a sumptuous star, mystical and red. Valmond saw it from his window, and knew it to be Parpon's watch-fire, by the grave of his brother Gabriel.

The chief procession started with the lighting of the bonfires. Singing softly, choristers and acolytes in robes, preceded the Curé, and devout believers and youths on horseback with ribbons flying, carried banners and shrines. Marshals kept the lines steady, and four were in constant attendance on a gorgeous carriage, all gilt and carving (the heirloom of the parish), in which reclined the figure of a handsome lad, impersonating John the Baptist, with long golden hair, dressed in rich robes and skins—a sceptre in his hand, a snowy lamb at his feet. The rude symbolism was softened and toned to an almost poetical refinement, and gave to the harmless revels a touch of Arcady.

After this semi-religious procession, nightfall brought the march of Garotte's Kalathumpians. They were carried on three long drays, each drawn by four horses, half of them white, half black. They were an outlandish crew of comedians, dressed after no pattern, save the absurd—clowns, satyrs, kings, soldiers, imps, barbarians. Many had hideous false faces, and a few horribly tall skeletons had heads of pumpkins with lighted candles inside. The marshals were pierrots and clowns on long stilts, who towered in a ghostly way above the crowd. They were cheerful, fantastic revellers, singing the maddest and silliest of songs, with singular refrains and repetitions.

They stopped at last in front of the Louis Quinze.

The windows of Valmond's chambers were alight, and to one a staff was fastened. Suddenly the Kalathumpians quieted where they stood, for the voice of their leader, a sort of fat king of Yvetot, cried out:

"See there, my noisy children!" It was the inventive limeburner who spoke. "What come you here for, my rollicking blades?"

"We are a long way from home; we are looking for our brother, your Majesty," they cried in chorus.

"Ha, ha! What is your brother like, jolly dogs?"

"He has a face of ivory, and eyes like torches, and he carries a silver sword."

"But what the devil is his face like ivory for, my fanfarons?"

"So that he shall not blush for us. He is a grand seigneur," they shouted back.

"Why are his eyes like torches, my ragamuffins?"

"To show us the way home."

Valmond appeared upon the balcony.

"What is it you wish, my comrades?" he asked.

"Brother," said the fantastic leader, "we've lost our way. Will you lead us home again?"

"It is a long travel," he answered, after the fashions of their own symbols. "There are high hills to climb; there may be wild beasts in the way, and storms come down the mountains."

"We have strong hearts, and you have a silver sword, brother."

"I cannot see your faces, to know if you are true, my children," he answered.

Instantly the clothes flew off, masks fell, pumpkins came crashing to the ground, the stilts of the marshals dropped, and thirty men stood upon the drays in crude military order, with muskets in their hands, and cockades in their caps. At that moment also, a flag — the tricolor — fluttered upon the staff out of Valmond's window. The roll of a drum came out of the street somewhere, and presently the people fell back before sixty armed men marching in columns, under Lagroin, while from the opposite direction came Lajeunesse with sixty others, silent all, till they reached the drays, and formed round them slowly.

Valmond stood motionless watching, and the people were very still, for this seemed like real life, and no comedy. Some of the soldiery had military clothes, old militia uniforms, or the rebel trappings of '37 ; others, less fortunate, wore their trousers in long boots, their coats buttoned lightly over their chests, and belted in ; and the Napoleonic cockade was in every cap.

"My children," said Valmond at last, "I see that your hearts are strong, and that you have the bodies of true men. We have sworn fealty to each other, and the badge of our love is in your caps. Let us begin our journey home. I will come down among you. I will come down among you, and I will lead you from Pontiac to the sea, gathering comrades as we go, then across the sea to France, then to Paris and the Tuileries, where the Bourbons usurp the place of a Napoleon."

He descended and mounted his waiting horse. At that moment Monsieur de la Rivière appeared on the balcony, and, stepping forward, said :

" My friends, do you know what you are doing ? This is folly. This man——"

He got no further, for Valmond raised his hand to Lagroin, and the drums began to beat. Then he rode down in front of Lajeunesse's men, the others sprang from the drays and fell into place, and soon the little army was marching, four deep, through the village.

This was the official beginning of Valmond's quest for empire. The people had a phrase, and they had a man ; and they saw no further than the hour.

As they filed past the house of Élise Malboir, the girl stood in the glow of a bonfire, beside the oven where Valmond had first seen her. All around her was the wide awe of night, enriched by the sweet perfume of a coming harvest. He doffed his hat to her, then to the tricolor, which Lagroin had fastened on a tall staff before the house. Élise did not stir, did not courtesy or bow, but stood silent—entranced. For she was in a dream. This man riding at the head of the simple villagers was part of her vision, and, at the moment, she did not rouse from the ecstasy of reverie where her new-born love had led her.

For Valmond the picture had a moving power. He heard again her voice crying in the smithy: " He is dying! Oh, my love ! my love !"

He was now in the heart of a fantastic adventure. Filled with its spirit, he would carry it bravely to the end, enjoying every step in it, comedy or tragedy. Yet all day, since he had eaten the holy bread, there had been ringing in his ears the words :

" Holy bread, I take thee ;
If I die suddenly,
Serve me as a sacrament."

It came home to him, at the instant, what a mad chance it all was. What was he doing ? No matter—it was all a game, in which nothing was sure—nothing save this girl. She would, he knew, with the abandon of an absorbing passion, throw all things away for him.

Such as Madame Chalice— Ah, she was a part of this brave fantasy, this dream of empire, this splendid play ! But Élise Malboir was actuality itself, true, absolute, abiding. His nature swam gloriously in this daring comedy ; he believed in it, he sank himself in it with a joyous recklessness; it was his victory or his doom. But it was a shake of the dice—had Fate loaded them against him ?

He looked up the hill toward the Manor. Life was there in its essence ; beauty, talent, the genius of the dreamer, like his own. But it was not for him ; dauphin or fool, it was not for him. Madame Chalice endured him for some talent he had shown, for the apparent sincerity of his love for the cause, but that was all. She was his inquisitor, but not his enemy. Yet she was ever in this dream of his, and he felt that she would always be ; the unattainable, the undeserved, more splendid than the cause itself, that for which he would give— what would he give ? Time would show.

But Élise Malboir, abundant, true, fine, in the healthy vigor of her nature, with no dream in her heart but love fulfilled—she was no part of his adventure, but of that vital spirit which can bring to the humblest as to the highest the good reality of life.

CHAPTER XI

IT was the poignancy of these feelings which, later, drew Valmond to the ashes of the fire in whose glow Élise had stood. The village was quieting down, the excited *habitants* had scattered to their homes. But in one or two houses there was dancing, and, as he passed, Valmond had heard the *chansons* of the humble games they played—primitive games, primitive *chansons:*

> " In my right hand I hold a rose-bush,
> Which will bloom, Manon lon la !
> Which will bloom in the month of May.
> Come into our dance, pretty rose-bush,
> Come and kiss, Manon lon la !
> Come and kiss whom you love best ! "

The ardor, the delight, the careless joy of youth were in the song and in the dance. These simple folk would marry, beget children, labor hard, obey Mother Church, and yield up the ghost peacefully in the end, after their kind ; but now and then there was born among them one not after their kind : even such as Madelinette Lajeunesse, with the stirring of talent in her veins, and the visions of the artistic temperament,—delight and curse all at once,—that lifted her out of the life, lonely, and yet sorrowfully happy.

Valmond looked around. How still and peaceful it was, the home of Élise standing apart in the quiet fields! The moon was lying off above the edge of mountains, looking out on the world complacently, as an indulgent janitor scans the sleepy street from his doorway. But involuntarily his eyes were drawn to the hill beyond, where showed a light in a window of the Manor. To-morrow he would go there: he had much to say to Madame Chalice.

He was abruptly drawn from his meditations by the entrance of Lagroin into the little garden. He followed the old man through the open doorway. All was dark, but as they stepped within they heard some one move; presently a match was struck, and Élise stepped forward with a candle raised level with her dusky head. Lagroin looked at her in indignant astonishment.

"Do you not see who is here, girl?" he demanded.

"Your Excellency," she said confusedly to Valmond, and, bowing, offered him a chair.

"You must pardon her, sire," said the old sergeant. "She has never been taught, and she's a wayward wench."

Valmond waved his hand. "Nonsense, we are friends. You are my general, she is your niece." His eyes followed her as she set out some cider for them, a small flask of cognac, and some seed-cakes; luxuries which were served but once a year in this house, as in most homes of Pontiac.

9

For a long time Valmond and Lagroin talked, devised, planned, schemed, till the old man grew husky and pale, and the sight of his senile weariness flashed the irony of the whole wild dream into Valmond's mind. He rose, and giving his arm, he led Lagroin to his bedroom, and bade him goodnight. When he returned to the room it was empty.

He looked around, and, seeing an open door, stepped to it quickly. It led into a little stairway.

He remembered then that there was a room which had been, apparently, tacked on, like an afterthought, to the end of the house. Seeing the glimmer of a light beyond, he went up a few steps, and came face to face with Élise, who, candle in hand, was about to descend the stairs again.

For a moment she stood quite still, then placed the candle on the rude little dressing-table, built of dry-goods boxes, and draped in fresh muslin. Valmond took in every detail of the chamber in a single glance. It was very simple and neat, with its small wooden bedstead corded with rope, the poor hickory rocking-chair, the flaunting chromo of the Holy Family, the sprig of blessed palm, the shrine of the Virgin, the print skirts hanging on the wall, the stockings lying across a chair, the bits of ribbon on the bed. The quietness, the alluring simplicity, the whole room filled with the rich presence of the girl, sent a flood of color to Valmond's face, and his heart beat hard. Curiosity only, had led him into the room, something more

vital held him there. Élise seemed to read his
thoughts, and, taking up her candle, she moved
toward the doorway. Neither had spoken. As
she was about to pass him, he suddenly touched
her arm. Glancing toward the window, he noticed
that the blind was not down. He turned, and
blew out the candle in her hand.

"Ah, your Excellency!" she cried in tremulous
affright.

"We could have been seen from outside,"
he explained. She turned and saw the moonlight
streaming in at the window, and lying like a
silver coverlet upon the floor. As if with a
blind, involuntary instinct for protection, she
stepped forward, and stood within it, motionless. The sight thrilled him, and he moved
towards her. The mind of the girl reasserted
itself, and she hastened to the door. Again, as
she was about to pass him, he put his hand upon
her shoulder.

"Élise, Élise!" he said. The voice was persuasive, eloquent, going to every far retreat of
emotion in her.

There was a sudden riot in his veins, and he
took her passionately in his arms, and kissed her
on the lips, on the eyes, on the hair, on the neck.
At that moment the outer door opened below, and
the murmur of voices came to them.

"Oh monsieur, oh monsieur, let me go," she
whispered fearfully. "It is my mother and
Duclosse the mealman."

Valmond recognized the fat, wheezy tones of Duclosse—Sergeant Duclosse. He released her, and she caught up the candle.

"What can you do?" she whispered.

"I will wait here. I must not go down," he replied. "It would mean ruin."

Ruin! ruin! Was she face to face with ruin already, she who, two minutes ago, was as safe and happy as a young bird in its nest? He saw instantly he had made a mistake, had been cruel, though he had not intended it.

"Ruin to me," he said at once. "Duclosse is a stupid fellow; he would not understand, he would desert me, and that would be disastrous at this moment. Go down," he said, "I will wait here, Élise."

Her brows knitted. "Oh monsieur, oh monsieur, I'd rather face death, I believe, than that you should remain here."

But he pushed her gently toward the door, and soon afterwards he heard her talking to Duclosse and her mother.

He sat down on the couch, and listened for a moment. His veins were still glowing from the wild moment just passed. Élise would come back—and then—what? She would be alone with him again in this room, loving him—fearing him. He remembered once how as a child he had seen a peasant strike his wife, felling her to the ground, and how afterwards she had clasped him round the neck and kissed him, as he bent over, in merely

vulgar fright lest he had killed her.   That scene
flashed before him.

Then came an opposing thought.   As Madame
Chalice had said, either as dauphin or fool, he was
playing a terrible game.   Why shouldn't he get
all he could out of it while it lasted—let the world
break over him when it must?   Why should he
stand in an orchard of ripe fruit, and refuse to pick
what lay luscious to his hand, what this stupid
mealman below would pick, and eat, and yawn
over?   There was the point.   Wouldn't the girl
rather have him, Valmond, at any price, than the
priest-blessed love of Duclosse and his kind?

The thought possessed, devoured him, for a
moment.   Suddenly there rang in his ears the
words which had haunted him all day :

" Holy bread, I take thee ;
    If I die suddenly,
    Serve me as a sacrament."

They passed back and forth in his mind for a
little time, before they had any significance.   Then
they gave birth to another thought.   Suppose he
stayed, suppose he took advantage of the love of
this girl?   He looked around the little room,
showing so peacefully in the moonlight—the religious symbols, the purity, the cleanliness, the calm
poverty.   He had known the inside of the boudoirs
and the bedchambers of women of fashion—he had
seen them, at least.   In them the voluptuous, the
indulgent, seemed part of the picture.   Good God!

He was not a beast that he could fail to see what this tiny bedroom would be, if he followed his wild will.

Some terrible fate might overtake his gay pilgrimage to empire, and leave him lost, abandoned, in a desert of ruin. Why not give up the adventure, and come to this quiet and this good peace, so shutting out the stir and violence of the world ?

All at once another face came into his thoughts, swam in his sight, and he knew that what he felt for this peasant girl was of one side of his nature only. All of him worth the having—was any worth the having ?—responded to that diffusing charm which brought so many men to the feet of the woman at the Manor, who had lovers by the score ; lovers who worshipped unrequited : from such as the Curé and the avocat, gentle and noble, to the young Seigneur, selfish and ulterior.

He got to his feet quietly. No, he would make a decent exit, in triumph or defeat, to honor this woman who was standing his friend. Let them, the British Government, proceed against him ; he would have only one trouble to meet, one to leave behind.

He would not load this poor girl with shame as well as sorrow. Her love itself was affliction enough to her. This adventure was serious ; a bullet might drop him ; the law might remove him : and so he would leave the girl alone.

He was about to descend by the window, when he heard a door shut below, and the thud of heavy steps outside the house. Drawing back, he waited until the footstep of Élise sounded upon the stair. She came in without a light, and at first did not see him. He heard her gasp. Stepping forward a little, he said :

"I am here, Élise. Come."

"Oh monsieur—your Excellency," she whispered affrightedly. "Oh, you cannot go down, for my mother sits ill by the fire. You cannot go out that way."

He took both her hands. "No matter. Poor child, you are trembling ! Come."

He drew her toward the couch. She shrank back. "Oh, no, monsieur, oh—I die of shame ! Oh monsieur ! "

"Do not be afraid, Élise," he answered gently, and drew her to his side. "Let us say good-night."

She grew very still, and he felt her move towards him, as she divined his purpose, and knew that this room of hers would have no shadow in it to-morrow, and her soul no unpardonable sin. A warm peace passed through her veins, and she drew nearer still. She did not know that this new ardent confidence came near to wrecking her. For Valmond had an instant's madness, and only saved himself from the tumult in his blood, by getting to his feet, with strenuous resolution. Taking both her hands, he kissed her on the cheeks, and said :

"Adieu, Élise, may your sorrow never be

more, and my happiness never be less. I am
going."

He felt her hand grasp his arm, as if with a
desire that he should not leave her. Then she
rose quickly, and came with him to the window.
Raising the sash, she held it, and he looked out.
There seemed to be no one in the road, no one in
the yard. So, half turning, he swung himself
down by his hands, and dropped to the ground.
From the window above a sob came to him, and
Élise's face showed for an instant in the moonlight, all tears.

He did not seek the road directly, but climbing
a fence near by, crossed a hayfield, going unseen,
as he thought, to the village.

But a woman, walking in the road with an old
gentleman, had seen and recognized him. Her
fingers clinched with anger at the sight, and her
spirit filled with disgust.

"What are you looking at?" said her compan-
ion, who was short-sighted.

"At the tricks moonlight plays with the eyes.
Shadows frighten me sometimes, my dear avocat."
She shuddered.

"My dear madame!" he said in warm sympathy.

CHAPTER XII

THE sun was going down behind the hills, like a drowsy boy to his bed, radiant and weary from his day's sport. The villagers were up at Dalgrothe Mountain soldiering for Valmond. Every evening, when the haymakers put up their scythes, the mill-wheel stopped turning, and the Angelus ceased, the men marched away into the hills, where the ardent " Napoleon " had pitched his camp.

Tents, muskets, ammunition came out of dark places, as they are ever sure to come when the war-trumpet sounds. All seems peace, but suddenly, at the wild call, the latent barbarian in human nature springs up and is ready ; and the cruder the arms the fiercer the temper that wields.

Recruits now arrived from other parishes, and besides those who came every night to drill, there were others who stayed always in camp. The limeburner left his kiln, and sojourned with his dogs at Dalgrothe Mountain, the mealman neglected his trade, and Lajeunesse was not to be found at his blacksmith shop, save after dark, when the red glow of his forge could be seen till midnight. He was captain of a company in the daytime, forgeron at night.

Valmond, no longer fantastic in dress, speech,

or manner, was happy, busy, buoyed up and cast down by turn, troubled, exhilarated. He could not understand these variations of health and mood. He had not felt equably well since the night of Gabriel's burial in the miasmic airs of the mountain. At times he felt a wonderful lightness of head and heart, with splendid hopes; again a heaviness and an aching, accompanied by a feeling of doom. He fought the depression, and appeared always before his men cheerful and alert. He was neither looking back nor looking forward, but living in his dramatic theme from day to day, and wondering if, after all, this movement, by some joyful, extravagant chance, might not carry him on even to the chambers of the Tuileries.

From the first day that he had gathered these peasants about him, had convinced, almost against their will, the wise men of the village, this fanciful adventure had been growing a deep reality to him. He had convinced himself; he felt that he could, in a larger sphere, gather thousands about him where he now gathered scores—with a good cause. Well, was his cause not good?

There were others to whom this growing reality was painful. The young Seigneur was serious enough about it, and more than once, irritated and perturbed, he sought Madame Chalice; but she gave him no encouragement, remarking coldly that Monsieur Valmond probably knew very well what he was doing, and was weighing all consequences.

She had become interested in a passing drama, and De la Rivière's attentions produced no impression on her, and gave her no pleasure. They were, however, not obtrusive. She had seen much of him two years before; he had been a good friend of her husband. She was amused at his attentions then : she had little to occupy her, and she felt herself superior to any man's emotions; not such as this young Seigneur could win her away from her passive but certain fealty. She had played with fire, from the very spirit of adventure in her, but she had not been burnt.

"You say he is an impostor, dear monsieur," she said languidly. "Do pray exert yourself, and prove him one. What is your evidence ? "

She leaned back in the very chair where she had sat looking at Valmond two weeks before, her fingers idly smoothing out the folds of her dress.

"Oh, the thing is impossible," he answered, blowing the smoke of a cigarette ; "we've had no real proof of his birth, and life—and so on."

" But there are relics !" she said suggestively, and she picked up the miniature of the Emperor.

"Owning a skeleton doesn't make it your ancestor," he answered.

He laughed, for he was pleased at his own cleverness, and he also wished to remain good-tempered.

"I am so glad to see you at last take the true attitude towards this," she responded brightly.

"If it's a comedy, enjoy it. If it's a tragedy—" she drew herself up with a little shudder, for she was thinking of that figure dropping from Élise's window—"you cannot stop it. Tragedy is inevitable ; it's only comedy that is within the gift and governance of mortals."

For a moment she was lost in the thought of Élise, of Valmond's vulgarity and commonness ; and he had dared to speak words of admiration to her ! She flushed to the hair, as she had done fifty times since she had seen him that moonlit night. Ah, she had thought him the dreamer, the enthusiast—maybe, in kind, credulous moments, the great man he claimed to be ; and he had only been the sensualist after all ! That he did not love Élise, she knew well enough ; he had been cold-blooded ; in this, at least, he was Napoleonic.

She had not spoken with him since that night, but she had had two long letters superscribed, "*In Camp, Headquarters, Dalgrothe Mountain*," and these had breathed only patriotism, the love of a cause, the warmth of a strong, virile temperament, almost a poetical abandon of unnamed ambitions and achievements. She had read the letters again and again, for she had found it hard to reconcile them with her later knowledge of this man. He wrote to her as to a confederate, frankly, warmly. She felt the genuine thing in him somewhere ; and, in spite of all, she had a sort of sympathy for him. Yet that scene—that scene ! She crimsoned with anger again, and, in spite of her smiling lips, the young Seigneur saw and wondered.

"The thing must end soon," he said, as he rose to go, for a messenger had come for him.   "He is injuring the peace, the trade, and the life of the parishes ; he is gathering men and arms, drilling, exploiting military designs in one country, to proceed against another.   England is at peace with France ! "

"An international matter, this ? " she asked sarcastically.

"Yes.   The Government at Quebec is English ; we are French, and he is French ; and I repeat, this thing is serious."

She smiled.   "I am an American.   I have no responsibility."

"They might arrest you for aiding and abetting if——"

"If what, dear and cheerful friend ? "

"If I did not make it right for you."   He smiled indulgently.

She touched his arm, and said with ironical sweetness :   "How you relieve my mind ! "   Then, with delicate insinuation :   "I have a lot of old muskets here, at least a hundred pounds of powder, and plenty of provisions, and I will send them to—Napoleon."

He instantly became grave.   "I warn you——"

She interrupted him.   "Nonsense !   You warn me ! "   She laughed mockingly.   "I warn you,

dear Seigneur, that you will be more sorry than
satisfied if you meddle in this matter."

"You are going to send those things to him ? "
he asked anxiously.

"Certainly—and food every day."

And she kept her word.

De la Rivière, as he went down the hill, thought
with irritation of how ill things were going with
him and Madame Chalice—so different from two
years ago, when their friendship had first begun.
He had remembered her with a singular persist-
ency, he had looked forward to her coming back,
and when she came, his heart had fluttered like a
school-boy's. But things had changed. Clearly,
she was interested in this impostor. Was it the
man himself or the adventure ? He did not know.
But the adventure was the man—and, who could
tell ? Once he thought he had detected some
warmth for himself in her eye, in the clasp of her
hand ; now——! A spirit of black, ungentle-
manly malignity seized upon him.

It possessed him most strongly at the moment
he was passing the home of Élise Malboir. The
girl was standing by the gate, looking towards
the village. Her brow was a little heavy, so that
it gave her eyes at all times a deep look, but now
De la Rivière saw that they were brooding as
well. There was a pathetic sadness in the poise
of the head. He did not take off his hat to her.

> " Oh, grand to the war he goes,
>   O gai, vive le roi ! "

he said teasingly.   He thought she might have a lover among the recruits at Dalgrothe Mountain.

She turned to him, startled, for she thought he meant Valmond.   She did not speak, but became very still and pale.

" Better tie him up with a garter, Élise, and get the old uncle back to Ville Bambord.   Trouble's coming.   The game 'll soon be up."

"What trouble ? " she faltered.

"Battle, murder, and sudden death," he answered and passed on with a sour laugh.

She slowly repeated his words, looked towards the Manor House with a strange expression, then went up to her little bedroom, and sat on the edge of the bed for a long time, where she had sat with Valmond.   Every word, every incident, of that night came back to her, and her heart filled up with worship.   It flowed over into her eyes, and fell upon her clasped hands.   If trouble did come to him ?—He had given her a new world, he should have her life and all else besides.

A half hour later De la Rivière came rapping at the Curé's door.   The sun was almost gone, the smell of the hayfields floated over the village, and all was quiet in the streets.   Women gossiped in their doorways, but there was no stir anywhere. With the young Seigneur was the member of the legislature for the county.   His mood was different from that of his previous visit to Pontiac, for he had been told that whether the cavalier adventurer was or was not a Napoleon, this campaign was illegal. He had made no move. Being a member of the legislature, he naturally shirked responsibility, and he had come to see the young Seigneur, who was justice of the peace, and practically mayor of the county. They found the Curé, the avocat, and Medallion, talking together.

The three were greatly distressed by the representations of the member, and Monsieur De la Rivière. The Curé turned to the avocat, inquiringly.

"The law, the law of the case is clear," he said helplessly. "If the peace is disturbed, if there is conspiracy to injure a country not at war with our own, if arms are borne with menace, if his Excellency——"

"His Excellency! my faith!—you're an ass, Garon!" cried the young Seigneur, with an angry sneer.

For once in his life the avocat bridled up. He got to his feet and stood silent an instant, raising himself up and down on his tip-toes, his lips compressed, his small body suddenly contracting to a firmness, and grown to a height, his eyelids working quickly. To the end of his life the Curé remembered and talked of the moment when the avocat gave battle. To him it was superb—he never could have done it himself.

"I repeat, *his Excellency*, Monsieur De la Rivière. My information is greater than yours, both by accident and through knowledge. I accept him as a Napoleon, and, as a Frenchman, I have no cause to blush for my homage, nor my faith, nor for his Excellency. He is a man of loving disposition, of great knowledge, of power to win men, of deep ideas, of large courage. Monsieur, I cannot forget the tragedy he stayed at the smithy, with risk of his own life. I cannot forget——"

The Curé, anticipating, nodded at him encouragingly. Probably the avocat intended to say something quite different, but the look in the Curé's eyes prompted him, and he continued :

" I cannot forget that he has given to the poor, and liberally to the Church, and has made and promised benefits to the deserving—ah, no, no, my dear Seigneur ! "

He had delivered his speech in a quaint, quick way, as though addressing a jury, and when he had finished, he sat down again, and nodded his head, and tapped his feet on the floor, and the Curé did the same, looking inquiringly at De la Rivière.

This was the first time there had been trouble in the little coterie. They had never differed painfully before. Tall Medallion longed to say something, but he waited for the Curé to speak.

"What have you to say, Monsieur le Curé ? " asked De la Rivière, testily.

" My dear friend Monsieur Garon has answered for us both," replied the Curé, quietly.

" Do you mean to say that you will not act with me to stop this thing," he urged, "not even for the safety of the people ? "

The reply was calm and resolute.

"My people shall have my prayers and my life, when needed, but I do not feel called upon to act for the state. I have the honor to be a friend of— his Excellency."

"By Heaven, the state shall act !" cried De la Rivière, fierce with rancour. "I shall go to this Valmond to-night, with my friend the member here. I shall warn him, and call upon the people to disperse. If he doesn't listen, let him beware ! I seem to stand alone in the care of Pontiac !"

The avocat turned to his desk. "No, no ; I will write you a legal opinion," he said with professional honesty. "You shall have my legal help ; but for the rest, I am one with my dear Curé."

"Well, Medallion, you, too ?" asked De la Rivière.

"I'll go with you to the camp," answered the auctioneer. "Fair play is all I care for. Pontiac will come out of this all right. Come along."

But the avocat kept them till he had written his legal opinion, and handed it courteously to the young Seigneur. They all were very silent. There had been a discourtesy, and it lay like a cloud on the coterie. De la Rivière opened the door to go out, after bowing to the Curé and the avocat, who stood up with mannered politeness, but presently turned, came back, was about to speak, when, catching sight of a miniature of Valmond on the avocat's desk, before which was set a bunch of violets, he wheeled and left the room without a word.

The moon had not yet risen, but stars were

shining, when the young Seigneur and the member came to Dalgrothe Mountain.   On one side of the Rock of Red Pigeons was a precipice and wild water ; on the other was a deep valley like a cup, and in the centre of this was a sort of plateau or gentle slope.   Dalgrothe Mountain towered above. Upon this plateau Valmond had pitched his tents. There was water, there was good air, and for pur-poses of drill—or defence—it was excellent.   The approaches were patrolled, so that no outside strag-glers could reach either the Rock of Red Pigeons or the valley, or see what was going on below, without permission.   Lagroin was everywhere, drilling, commanding, brow-beating his recruits one minute, and praising them the next, and Lajeunesse, Garotte, Muroc, and Duclosse were invaluable, each after his kind.

The young Seigneur and his companions passed unchallenged, on up to the Rock of Red Pigeons. Looking down, they had a perfect view of the encampment.   The tents had come from lumber-camps, from river-driving gangs, and from private stores ; there was no regular uniform, but flags were flying everywhere, many fires were burning, the voice of Lagroin in command came up the valley loudly, and Valmond sat on his horse watching the drill and a march past.   The fires lit up the sides of the valley and glorified the mountains beyond.   In this inspiring air it was impossible to feel an accent of disaster or the stealthy footfall of ruin.

The three came down into the valley, then up onto the plateau, where they were challenged, allowed to pass, and came to where Valmond sat upon his horse. At sight of them, with a suspicion of the truth, he ordered Lagroin to march the men down the long plateau. They made a good figure filing past the three visitors, as the young Seigneur admitted.

Valmond dismounted, and waited for them. He looked weary, and there were dark circles round his eyes, as though he had an illness ; but he stood erect and dignified. His uniform was that of a general of the Empire. It was rather dingy, yet it was of rich material, and he wore the ribbon of the Legion of Honor on his breast. His paleness did not arise from fear, for when his eyes met Monsieur De la Rivière's there was in them waiting inquiry,—nothing more. He greeted them all politely, and Medallion warmly, shaking his hand twice, for he knew well that the gaunt auctioneer had only kindness in his heart, and they had exchanged humorous stories more than once—a friendly bond.

He motioned to his tent near by, but the young Seigneur declined.

" It is business, and imperative," he said. Valmond bowed. " Isn't it time this comedy was finished ? " continued De la Rivière, waving his hand towards the encampment.

" My presence here is my reply," answered Valmond. " But how does it concern monsieur ? "

" All that concerns Pontiac concerns me."

" And me ; I am as good a citizen as you."

" You are troubling our people. This is illegal —this bearing arms, these purposes of yours. It is mere filibustering, and you are an——"

Valmond waved his hand, as if to stop the word. "I am Valmond Napoleon, monsieur."

" If you do not promise to drop this, I will arrest you," said De la Rivière, sharply.

" You ? " Valmond smiled ironically.

" I am a justice of the peace. I have the power."

" I have the power to prevent arrest, and I will prevent it, monsieur. You alone of all this parish, I believe of all this province, turn a sour face, a sour heart to me. I regret it, but I do not fear it."

" I will have you in custody, or there is no law in Quebec."

Valmond's face had become a feverish red, and he made an impatient gesture. Both men were filled with bitterness, for both knew well that the touchstone of this malice was Madame Chalice. Hatred looked out of their eyes. It was, each knew, a fight to the dark end.

" There is not law enough to justify you, monsieur," answered Valmond, quickly.

" Be persuaded, monsieur," said the member to Valmond, with a smirking gesture.

" All this country could not persuade me ; only France can do that, and first I shall persuade France," he answered.

"Mummer!" broke out De la Rivière. "By Heaven, I will arrest you now!"

He stepped forward, putting his hand in his breast, as if to draw a weapon, though, in truth, it was a summons.

Like lightning the dwarf shot in between, and a sword flashed up at De la Rivière's breast.

"I saved your father's life, but I will take yours, if you step farther, dear Seigneur," he said coolly.

Valmond had not stirred, but his face had become pale again.

"That will do, Parpon," he said quietly. "Monsieur had best go," he added to De la Rivière, "or even his beloved law may not save him!"

"I will put an end to this," cried the other, bursting with anger. "Come, gentlemen," he said to his companions, and turned away.

Medallion lingered behind the others.

"Your Excellency, if ever you need me, let me know. I'd do much to prove myself no enemy," he said.

Valmond gave him his hand gratefully, bowed, and beckoning a soldier to take his horse, walked towards his tent. He swayed slightly as he went, then a trembling seized him. He staggered as he entered the door of the tent, and Parpon, seeing him, ran forward, and caught him in his arms. The little man laid him down, felt his pulse, his heart, saw the dark stain on his lips, and cried out in a great fear:

"My God!   The black fever!   Ah, my Napoleon!"

For hours Valmond lay in a burning stupor,
and word went abroad that he might die ; but
Parpon insisted that all would be well presently,
and as no one but the Little Chemist and the Curé
were permitted to come in or near the tent, his
anxious followers were fain to content themselves
with the dwarf's assurance of his recovery.

CHAPTER XIII

THE sickness had come like a whirlwind : when it passed, what would be left ? The fight went on in the quiet hills—a man of no great stature or strength, against a monster who racked him in a fierce embrace. A thousand scenes flashed through Valmond's brain, before his eyes, while the great wheel of torture went round, and he was broken, broken,—mended and broken again, upon it. Spinning—he was forever spinning, like a tireless moth through a fiery air, and the world went roaring past. In vain he cried to the wheelman to stop the wheel : there was no answer. Would those stars never cease blinking in and out, nor the wind stop whipping the swift clouds past ? So he went on, endless years, driving through space, some terrible intangible weight dragging at his heart, and all his body panting as it spun.

Grotesque faces came and went, and bright-eyed women floated by, laughing at him, beckoning to him ; but he could not come, because of this tireless going. He heard them singing, he felt the divine notes in his battered soul ; he tried to weep for the hopeless joy of it ; but the tears came no higher than his throat. Why did they mock him so ? At last, all the figures merged into one, and she had the face—ah, he had known it well, centuries ago !—of Madame Chalice. Strange that she was so young still, and that was so long past —when he stood on a mountain, and, clambering a high wall of rock, looked over into a happy No-man's Land.

Why did the face elude him so, flashing in and out of the vapors ? Why was its look sorrowful and distant ? And yet there was that perfect smile, that adorable aspect of the brow, that light in the deep eyes. He tried to stop the eternal spinning, but it went remorselessly on ; and presently the face was gone ; but not till it had given him ease of his pain.

Then came fighting, fighting, nothing but fighting—endless charges of cavalry, continuous wheelings, and advancings, and retreatings, and the mad din of drums ; afterwards, in a swift quiet, the deep, even thud of horses' hoofs striking the ground. Flags and banners flaunted gayly by. How the helmets flashed, and the foam flew from the bits ! But those flocks of blackbirds flying over the heads of the misty horsemen—they made him shiver. Battle, battle, battle, and death, and being born—he felt it all.

Suddenly there came a wide peace and clearing, and the everlasting jar and movement ceased. Then a great pause, and light streamed round him, comforting him.

It seemed to him that he was lying helpless and still by falling water in a valley. The water

soothed him, and he fell asleep. After a long
time he waked, and dimly knew that a face, good
to look at, was bending over him. In a vague,
far-off way he saw that it was Élise. Malboir;
but, even as he knew this, his eyes closed, the
world dropped away, and he sank to sleep
again.

It was no fantasy or delirium; for Élise had
come. She had knelt beside his bed, and given
him drink, and smoothed his pillow; and once,
when no one was in the tent, she stooped and
kissed his hot dark lips, and whispered words
that were not for his ears to hear, nor to be heard
by any of this world. The good Curé found her
there. He had not heart to bid her go home,
and he made it clear to the villagers that he
approved of her great kindness. But he bade
her mother come also, and she stayed in a tent
near by.

Lagroin and sixty men held the encampment,
and every night the recruits came from the village,
drilled as before, and waited for the fell disease
to pass. None knew its exact nature, but now
and again, in long years, some one going to
Dalgrothe Mountain was seized by it, and died,
or was left stricken with a great loss of the senses
or the limbs. Yet once or twice, they said, men
had come up from it no worse at all. There
was no known cure, and the Little Chemist could
only watch the swift progress of the fever, and use
simple remedies to allay the suffering. Parpon

guessed that the disease had seized upon Valmond the night of the burial of Gabriel. He remembered now the sickly, pungent air that floated past, and how Valmond, weak from the loss of blood in the fight at the smithy, shuddered, and drew his cloak about him. A few days would end it, for good or ill.

Madame Chalice received the news with consternation, and pity would have sent her to Valmond's bedside, but that she had heard that Élise was his faithful nurse and servitor. This fixed in her mind the belief that if Valmond died he would leave both misery and shame behind ; and that if he lived she should, in any case, see him no more. But she sent wines and delicacies to him, and despatched a messenger to a city sixty miles away, for the best physician. Then she sought the avocat to find whether he had any exact information as to Valmond's friends in Quebec or in France. She had promised not to be his enemy, and she remembered with a sort of sorrow that she had even let him believe that she meant to be his friend ; and, having promised, she would help him in his sore strait.

She had heard of De la Rivière's visit to Valmond, and she intended sending for him, but delayed it. The avocat told her nothing ; matters were in abeyance, and she abided the issue ; meanwhile getting news of the sick man twice a day. But she used all her influence to keep up the feeling for him in the parish, to prevent flagging of enthusiasm. This she did out of a large heart, and a kind of loyalty to her own temperament and to his ardor for his cause. Until he was proved the comedian (in spite of the young Seigneur) she would stand by him, so far as his public career was concerned. Misfortune could not make her turn from a man; it was then she gave him a helping hand. After all, what was between him and Élise was for their own souls and consciences.

As she passed the little cottage in the fields the third morning of Valmond's illness, she saw the girl entering. Élise had come to get some necessaries for Valmond and for her mother. She was very pale; her face had gained a spirituality, a refinement, new and touching. Madame Chalice was tempted to go and speak to her, and started to do so, but turned back.

"No, no, not until we know the worst of this illness—then!" she said to herself.

But ten minutes later De la Rivière was not so kind. He had guessed a little at Élise's secret, and as he passed the house on the way to visit Madame Chalice, seeing the girl, he stopped at her door and said:

"How is the distinguished gentleman, Élise? I hear you are his slave."

The girl turned a little pale. She was passing a hot iron over some coarse sheets, and pausing, she looked steadily at him and replied:

"It is not far to Dalgrothe Mountain, monsieur."

"The journey's too long for me ; I haven't your hot young blood," he said coarsely.

"It was not so long a dozen years ago, monsieur."

De la Rivière flushed to his hair.   That memory was a bitter chapter in his life—a boyish folly, which involved the miller's wife.   He had buried it, the village had forgotten it,—such of it as knew, —and the remembrance of it stung him.   He had, however, brought it on himself, and he must eat the bitter fruit.

The girl's eyes were cold and hard.   She knew him to be Valmond's enemy, and she had no idea of sparing him.   She knew also that he had been courteous enough to send a man each day to in-quire after Valmond, but that was not to the point ; he was torturing her, he had prophesied the downfall of her "spurious Napoleon."

"It will be too long a journey for you, and for all presently," he said.

"You mean that his Excellency will die ? " she asked, her heart beating so hard that it hurt her. Yet the flat-iron moved backwards and forwards upon the sheets mechanically.

"Or fight a Government," he answered.   "He has had a good time, and good times can't last forever, can they, Élise ?   Have you ever thought of that ? "

She gasped for breath and swayed over the table. In an instant he was beside her ; for, though he had been irritable and ungenerous, he had at bottom a kind heart. Catching up a glass of water, he ran an arm round her waist, and held the cup to her lips.

"What's the matter, my girl?" he asked. "There, pull yourself together."

She drew away from him, though grateful for his new attitude. She could not bear everything. She felt nervous and strangely weak.

"Won't you go, monsieur?" she said, and turned to her ironing again.

He looked at her closely, and not unkindly. For a moment the thought possessed him, that evil and ill had come to her. But he put it away from him, for there was that in her eyes which gave his quick suspicions the lie. He guessed, however, that the girl loved Valmond, and he left her with that thought. Going up the hill, deep in meditation, he called at the Manor, to find that Madame Chalice was absent, and would not be back till evening.

When Élise was alone, a weakness seized her again, as it had done when De la Rivière was present. She had had no sleep in four days, and it was wearing on her, she told herself, refusing to believe that a sickness was coming. She went up to her little bedroom, and, leaning against the open window, figured Valmond in her mind, as he stood in this place and that, his voice, his words to her, the look in his face, the clasp of his hand.

All at once she fell on her knees before the little shrine of the Virgin, and burst into tears. Her

rich hair, breaking loose, flowed round her—the
picture of a Magdalen ; but it was, in truth, a
pure girl with an honest heart.   At last she
calmed herself and began to pray :

"Ah, dear Mother of God, thou who dost speak
for the sorrowful before thy Son and the Father, be
merciful to me and hear me.   I am but a poor girl,
and my life is no matter.   But he is a great man,
and he has work to do, and he is true and kind, and
he loves thy Son.   Oh, pray for him, divine Mother,
sweet Mary, that he may be saved from death.
If the cup must be emptied, may it be given to me
to drink ! Oh, see how all the people come to him
and love him !   For the saving of Madelinette,
oh, may his own life be given him !   He cannot
pray for himself, but I pray for him.   Dear Mother
of God, I love him, and I would lose my life for
his sake.   Sweet Mary, comfort thy child, and
out of thy own sorrow be good to my sorrow.
Hear me and pray for me, divine Mary !   Amen."

Her whole nature emptied itself into this fervid
petition, and there came upon her a strange calm-
ness and clearness of brain, exhausted in body as
she was.

"Madame Dégardy ! Madame Dégardy !" she
cried with sudden inspiration as she rose to her
feet.   "Ah, I will find her ; she may save him
with her herbs !" and hurrying out of the house
and down through the village, she sought the little
hut by the river, where the old woman lived.

Élise had been to Madame Dégardy as good a

friend, as a half-mad creature, with no memory,
would permit her. Parpon had lived for years
in the same village, but, though he was her own
son, she had never given him a look of recognition,
had used him as she used all others. In turn, the
dwarf had never told any one but Valmond of the
relationship, and so the two lived their strange
lives in their own singular way. But the Curé knew
who it was that kept the old woman's house sup-
plied with wood and other necessaries during the
long winters. Parpon himself had tried to summon her to Valmond's bedside, for he knew well
her skill with herbs, but the little hut was empty,
and he could get no trace of her. She had disap-
peared the night Valmond was seized of the fever,
and she came back to her little home in the very
hour that Élise visited her. The girl found her
boiling some savory mess before a big fire. She
was stirring the pot diligently, now and then
sprinkling in what looked like a brown dust, and
watching the brew intently.

She nodded, but did not look at Élise, and said
crossly :

"Come in, come in, and shut the door, silly."

"Madame," said the girl, "his Excellency has
the black fever."

"What of that?" returned the old woman,
irritably.

"I thought maybe your herbs could cure him.
You've cured others, and this is an awful sickness.
Ah, won't you save him, if you can?"

" What are you to him, pale face ? " she said, her eyes peering into the pot.

" Nothing more to him than you are, madame," the girl answered wearily.

" I'll cure because I want, not because you ask me, pretty brat."

Élise's heart gave a leap : these very herbs that were brewing were for Valmond ! The old woman had travelled far to get the medicaments immediately she had heard of Valmond's illness. Night and day she had trudged, and she was more brown and weather-beaten than ever.

"The black fever ! the black fever ! " she cried. "I know it well. It's most like a plague. I know it. But I know the cure—ha, ha ! Come along now, feather-legs, what are you staring there for ? Hold that jug while I pour the darling liquor in. Ha, ha ! Crazy Joan hasn't lived for nothing. They have to come to her ; the great folks have to come to her."

So she meandered on, while filling the jug, and in the warm dusk they travelled up to Dalgrothe Mountain, and came to Valmond's tent. By the couch knelt Parpon, watching the labored breathing of the sick man. When he saw Madame Dégardy, he gave a growl of joy, and instantly made way for her. She pushed him back with her stick contemptuously, looked Valmond over, ran her fingers down his cheek, felt his throat, and at last held his restless hand. Élise, with the quick intelligence of love, stood ready. The old woman

11

caught the jug from her, swung it into the hollow
of her arm, poured the cup half full, and motioned
the girl to lift up Valmond's head. Élise raised it
to her bosom, bending her face down close to his.
Madame Dégardy instantly pushed back her head.

" Don't get his breath—that's death, idiot ! "
she said, and began to slowly pour the liquid into
Valmond's mouth. It was a tedious process at
first, but at length he began to swallow naturally,
and finished the cup.

For an hour there was no change, and then he
became less restless. After another cupful, his
eyes half opened. Within another hour a per-
spiration came, and he was very quiet, and sleeping restfully. Parpon crouched near the door,
watching it all with deep piercing eyes. Madame
Dégardy never moved from her place, but stood
shaking her head and muttering. At last Lagroin
came, and whisperingly asked after his master ;
then seeing him in a healthy and peaceful sleep,
he stooped and kissed the hand lying upon the
blanket.

" Beloved sire ! Thank the good God ! " he
said.

Soon after he had gone, there was a noise of
tramping about the tent, and then a suppressed
cheer, which was fiercely stopped by Parpon, and
the soldiers of the Household Troops scattered to
their tents.

" What's that ? " asked Valmond, opening his
eyes bewilderedly.

" Your soldiers, sire," answered the dwarf.

Valmond smiled languidly. Then he saw Madame Dégardy and Élise.

" I am very sleepy, dear friends," he said with a courteous, apologetic gesture, and closed his eyes.

Presently they opened again. " My snuff-box—in my pocket," he said to the old woman, waving a hand to where his uniform hung from the tent-pole ; " it is for you, madame."

She understood, smiled grimly, felt in a waistcoat pocket, found the snuff-box, and squatting on the ground like a tailor, she took two pinches, and sat holding the enamelled silver box in her hand.

" Crazy Joan's no fool, dear lad," she said at last, and took another pinch, and nodded her head again and again, while he slept soundly.

CHAPTER XIV

" LIGHTS out !"

The bugle rang softly down the valley, echoed away tenderly in the hills, and was lost in the distance.

Roused by the clear call, Élise rose from watching beside Valmond's couch and turned towards the door of the tent. The spring of a perfect joy at his safety had been followed by an aching in all her body and a trouble at her heart. Her feet were like lead, her spirit quivered and shrank by turn. The light of the camp-fires sent a glow through the open doorway upon the face of the sleeper.

She leaned over him. The look she gave him seemed to her anxious spirit like a farewell. This man had given her a new life, and out of this had come a new sight. Valmond had escaped death, but in her poor confused way she felt another storm gathering about him. A hundred feelings possessed her; but one thought was master of them all: when trouble drew round him she must be near him, must be strong to help him, protect him, if need be. Yet a terrible physical weakness was on her. Her limbs trembled, and her heart throbbed in a sickening way.

Valmond stirred in his sleep; a smile passed over his face. She wondered what gave it birth. She knew well it was not for her, that smile. It belonged to his dream of success—when a thousand banners should flaunt in the gardens of the Tuileries. Overmastered by a sudden rush of emotion, she fell on her knees at his bed-side, bursting into noiseless sobs which shook her from head to foot. Every nerve in her body responded to the shock of feeling; she was having her dark hour alone.

At last, staggering to her feet, she turned to the open door. The tents lay silent in the moonshine, but wayward lights flickered in the sumptuous dusk, and the quiet of the hills hung like a canopy over the bivouac of the little army. No token of misfortune came out of this peaceful encampment, no omen of disaster crossed the long lane of drowsy fires and huge amorous shadows. The sense of doom was in the girl's own heart, not in this deep cradle of the hills.

Now and again a sentinel crossed the misty line of vision, silent, and majestically tall, in the soft haze which came down from Dalgrothe Mountain, and fell like a delicate silver veil before the face of the valley.

As she looked, lost in a kind of dream, there floated up from a distant tent the refrain she knew so well:

> " Oh, say, where goes your heart ?
> *O gai, vive le roi !*"

Her hand caught her bosom as if to stifle a sudden pain. That song had been the keynote to her new life, and it seemed now as if it were also to be the final benediction. All her spirit gathered itself up for a great resolution: she would not yield to this invading weakness, this misery of body and mind.

Someone drew out of the shadows and came towards her. It was Madame Dégardy. She had seen the sobbing figure inside the tent, but with the occasional wisdom of the foolish of this world, she had not been less considerate than the children of light.

With brusque, kindly taps of her stick, she drove the girl to her own tent, and bade her sleep; but sleep was not for Élise that night, and in the gray dawn, while yet no one was stirring in the camp, she passed slowly down the valley to her home.

Madame Chalice was greatly troubled also. Valmond's life was saved. In two days he was on his feet, eager and ardent again, and preparing to go to the village : but what would the end of it all be ? She knew of De la Rivière's intentions, and she foresaw a crisis. If Valmond were in very truth a Napoleon, all might be well, though this great adventure must close here. If he were an impostor, things would go cruelly hard with him. Impostor ? Strange, how, in spite of all evidence against him, she still felt a sureness in him somewhere ; a radical reality, a convincing quality of presence. At times he seemed like an

actor playing his own character.   She could never
quite get rid of that feeling.

In her anxiety, for she was in the affair for good
or ill, she went again to Monsieur Garon.

" You believe in Monsieur Valmond, dear avocat ? " she asked.

The little man looked at her admiringly, though
his admiration was a quaint, Arcadian thing ;
and, perching his head on one side abstractedly,
he answered :

" Ah, yes, ah, yes ! Such candor ! He is the
son of Napoleon and a princess, born after Napoleon's fall, not long before his death."

" Then Monsieur Valmond is really nameless ? " she asked.

" Ah, there is the point—the only point ; but
his Excellency can clear up all that, and will do so
in good time, he says.   He maintains that France
will accept him."

" But the government here, will they put him
down ? proceed against him ?   Can they ? "

" Ah, yes, I fear they can proceed against him.
He may recruit men, but he may not drill and
conspire—and so on.   Yet "—the old man smiled,
as though at some distant and pleasing prospect—
"the cause is a great one; it is great.   Ah, madame,
dear madame "—he got to his feet, and stepped into
the middle of the floor—"he has the true Napoleonic
spirit. He loves it all. At the very first, it seemed
as if he were going to be a little ridiculous ; now it
is as if there was but one thing for him—love of

France, and loyalty to the cause. Ah, think of the glories of the Empire : of France as the light of Europe, of Napoleon making her rich, and proud, and dominant. And think of her now, sinking into the wallow of bourgeois vulgarity. If—if, as his Excellency said, the light were to come from here, even from this far corner of the world, from this old France, to be the torch of freedom once again —from our little parish here ! "

His face was glowing, his thin hands made a quick gesture of charmed anticipation.

Madame Chalice looked at him in a sort of wonder and delight. Dreamers all ! And this visionary Napoleon had come into the little man's quiet, cultured, passive life, and had transformed him, filled him with adventure and patriotism. There must be something behind Valmond, some real, even some great thing, or this were not possible. It was not surprising that she, with the spirit of dreams and romance deep in her, should be sympathetic, even carried away for the moment.

" How is the feeling in the parish since his illness ? " she asked.

" Never so strong as now. Many new recruits come to him. Organization goes on, and his Excellency has issued a proclamation. I have advised him against that—it is not necessary, it is illegal. He should not tempt our Government too far. But he is a man of as great simplicity as courage, of directness and virtue—a wholesome soldier——"

She thought again of that moonlit night, and
Élise's window, and a kind of hatred of the man
came up in her.   No, no, they all were wrong, he
was not the true thing.

"Dear avocat," she said suddenly, "you are a
good friend.   May I always have as good!   But
have you ever thought that this thing may end in
sore disaster ?   Is the man worthy our friendship
and our adherence ?   Are we doing right ?"

"Ah, dear madame, convictions, principles,
truth, they lead to good ends—somewhere.   I
have a letter here from Monsieur Valmond.   It
breathes noble things ; it has humor, too—ah,
yes, so quaint!   I am to see him this afternoon.
He returns to the Louis Quinze to-day.   The Curé
and I——"

She laid her hand on his arm, interrupting
him.   "Will you take me this evening to Monsieur Valmond, dear friend ?" she asked.

She saw now how useless it was to attempt anything through these admirers of Valmond; she
must do it herself.   He must be firmly warned
and dissuaded.   The conviction had suddenly come
to her with great force, that the end was near—
come to her as it came to Élise.   Her wise
mind had seen the sure end; the heart of the
peasant girl had felt it.

The avocat readily promised.   She was to call
for him at a little before eight o'clock.   But she
decided that she would first seek Élise ; before
she accused the man, she would question the

woman. Above and beyond all anger she felt at this miserable episode, there was pity in her heart for the lonely girl.

Madame Chalice was capable of fierce tempers, of great caprices, of even wild injustice, when her emotions had their way with her ; but her heart was large, her nature deep and broad, and her instincts kind. The little touch of barbarism in her gave her, too, a sense of primitive justice. She was self-analytical, critical of life and conduct, yet her mind and her heart, when put to the great test, were above mere analysis.

Her rich nature, alive with these momentous events, feeling the prescience of coming crisis, sent a fine glow into her face, into her eyes. Excitement gave a fresh elasticity to her step. In spite of her serious thoughts, she looked very young, almost irresponsible. No ordinary observer could guess the mind that lay behind the glowing eyes. Even the tongue at first deceived, till it began to probe, to challenge, to drop sharp, incisive truths in little gold-leaved pellets, which brought conviction when the gold-leaf wore off.

The sunlight made her part of the brilliant landscape, and she floated into it, neither too dainty nor too luxurious. The greatest heat of the day was past, and she was walking slowly under the maples, on the way to Élise's home, when she was arrested by a voice near her. Then a tall figure leaped the fence, and came to her with outstretched hand and an unmistakable smile of pleasure.

"I've called at the Manor twice, and found you out, so I took to the highway," he said gayly.

"My dear Seigneur," she answered with mock gravity, "ancestors' habits show in time."

"Come, that's severe, isn't it ? "

"You have waylaid me in a lonely place, master highwayman !" she said with a torturing sweetness.

He had never seen her so radiantly debonair ; yet her heart was full of annoying anxiety.

"There's so much I want to say to you," he answered more seriously.

"So very much ? "

"Very much indeed."

She looked up the road. "I can give you ten minutes," she said. "Suppose we walk up and down under these trees. It's shady and quiet here. Now, proceed, monsieur. Is it my money or my life ? "

"You are in a charming mood to-day."

"Which is more than I could say for you the last time we met. You threatened, stormed, were childish, impossible to a degree."

His face became grave. "We were such good friends once," he said softly.

"Once—once ? " she asked maliciously. "Once Cain and Abel were a happy family. When was that once, Monsieur De la Rivière ? "

"Two years ago. What talks we had then !

And I had so looked forward to your coming again. It was the alluring thing in my life, your arrival," he went on ; "but something came between."

His tone nettled her. He talked as if he had some distant claim on her.

"Something came between," she repeated slowly, mockingly. "That sounds melodramatic indeed. What was it came between—a coach-and-four, or a grand army ? "

" Nothing so stately," he answered, piqued by her tone. " A filibuster and his ragamuffins."

"*Ragamuffins* would be appreciated by Monsieur Valmond's followers, spoken at the four corners," she answered.

" Then I'll change it," he said : " a ragamuffin and his filibusters."

" The 'ragamuffin' always speaks of his enemies with courtesy, and the filibusters love their leader," was her tart rejoinder.

" At half a dollar a day," he answered sharply.

" They get that much from his Excellency, do they ? " she asked in real surprise. " That doesn't look like filibustering, does it ? "

" 'His Excellency'!" he retorted. " Why won't you look this matter straight in the face ? Napoleon, or no Napoleon, the end of this thing is ruin."

"Take care that you don't get lost in the débris," she said bitingly.

"I can take care of myself. I am sorry to have you mixed up in it."

"You are sorry! How good of you! How paternal!"

"If your husband were here——"

"If my husband were here, you would probably be his best friend," she rejoined with acid sweetness; "and I should still have to take care of myself."

Had he no sense of what was possible to leave unsaid to a woman? She was very angry, though she was also a little sorry for him; for perhaps in the long run he would be in the right. But he must pay for his present stupidity.

"You wrong me," he answered with a quick burst of feeling. "You are most unfair. You punish me because I do my public duty; and because I would do anything in the world for you, you punish me the more. Have you forgotten two years ago? Is it so easy to your hand, a true and constant admiration, a sincere homage, that you throw it aside like—— ?"

"Monsieur De la Rivière," she said with exasperating deliberation, her eyes filling with a dangerous light, "your ten minutes is more than up. And it has been quite ten minutes too long."

"If I were a filibuster——" he said bitterly and suggestively.

She interrupted him, murmuring with a purring softness: "If you had only courage enough——!"

He waved his hand angrily. "If I had, I should hope you would prove a better friend to me than you are to this man."

" Ah, in what way do I fail toward ' this man '? "

"By encouraging his downfall. See—I know I am taking my life in my hands, as it were, but I tell you this thing will do you harm when it goes abroad."

She felt the honesty of his words, though they angered her. He seemed to impute some personal interest in Valmond. She would not have it from any man in the world.

"If you will pick up my handkerchief—ah, thank you ! We must travel different roads in this matter. You have warned ; let me prophesy : Monsieur Valmond—Napoleon will come out of this with more honor than yourself."

"Thanks to you, then," he said gallantly, for he admired her very stubbornness.

"Thanks to himself. I honestly believe that you will be ashamed of your part in this, one day."

"In any case, I will force the matter to a conclusion," he answered firmly. "The fantastic thing must end."

"When ? "

"Within two or three days."

"When all is over, perhaps you will have the honesty to come and tell me which was right—you or I. Good-by."

He watched her sulkily as she left him, dipping her parasol in mocking salutation, and turned her steps towards the Malboir cottage.

Élise was busy at her kitchen fire. She looked up, nervously, as her visitor entered. Her heavy brow grew heavier, her eyes gleamed sulkily, as she dragged herself wearily forward, and stood silent and resentful. Why had this lady of the Manor, come to her ?

Madame Chalice scarcely knew how to begin, for in truth, she wanted to be the girl's friend, and she feared making her do, or say some wild thing.

She looked round the quiet room. A pot of fruit was boiling on the stove, giving out a fragrant savor, and Élise's eye was on it mechanically. A bit of sewing lay across a chair, and on the wall hung a military suit of the old sergeant, beside it a short sabre. An old tricolor was draped from a beam, and one or two maps of France were pinned on the wall. She fastened her look on the maps. They seemed to be her cue.

"Have you any influence with your uncle ? " she asked.

Élise did not answer.

"Because," Madame Chalice went on smoothly, ignoring her silence, "I think it would be better for him to go back to Ville Bambord—I am sure of it."

The girl's lip curled angrily. What right had this great lady to interfere with her or hers ? What did she mean ?

"My uncle is a general and a brave man ; he can take care of himself," she answered defiantly.

Madame Chalice did not smile at the title. She

admired the girl's courage. She persisted, however.

"He is one man, and——"

"He has plenty of men, madame, and his Excellency——"

"His Excellency and hundreds of men cannot
stand if the Government send soldiers against
them."

"Why should the Gover'ment do that? They're
only going to France; they mean no trouble
here."

"They have no right to drill and conspire here,
my girl."

"Well, my uncle and his men will fight; we'll
all fight," Élise retorted, her hands grasping the
arms of the rocking-chair she sat in.

"But why shouldn't we avoid fighting? What
is there to fight for? You are all very happy here.
You were very happy here before Monsieur Valmond came. Are you happy now?"

Madame Chalice's eyes searched the flushed
face anxiously. She was growing more eager
every moment to serve, if she could, this splendid
creature.

"We would die for him!" answered the girl,
quickly.

"*You* would die for him," she said slowly and
meaningly.

"And what's it to you, if I would?" came the
sharp retort. "Why do you fine people meddle
yourselves with poor folks' affairs?"

Then, remembering she was a hostess, with the instinctive courtesy of her race, she said : " Ah, pardon, madame ; you . meant nothing, I'm sure."

" Why should fine folk make poor folk unhappy ? " said Madame Chalice, quietly and sorrowfully, for she saw that Élise was suffering, and all the woman in her came to her heart and lips. She laid her hand on the girl's arm. " Indeed yes, why should fine folk make poor folk unhappy ? It is not I alone who make you unhappy, Élise."

.The girl shook off the hand resentfully, for she guessed the true significance of Madame Chalice's words.

" What are you trying to find out ? " she asked fiercely. " What do you want to do ? Did I ever come in your way ? Why do you come into mine ? What's my life to you ? Nothing, nothing at all. You're here to-day and away to-morrow. You're English ; you're not of us. Can't you see that I want to be left alone ? If I were unhappy I could look after myself. But I'm not, I'm not. I tell you I'm not. I'm happy. I never knew what happiness was till now. I'm so happy that I can stand here and not insult you, though you've insulted me."

" I meant no insult, Élise. I want to help you ; that is all. I know how hard it is to confide in one's relatives, and I wish with all my heart I might be your friend, if you ever need me."

12

The girl met her sympathetic look clearly and steadily.

"Speak plain to me, madame," she said.

"Élise, I saw some one climb out of your bedroom window," was the slow reply.

"Oh, my God! oh, my God!" she cried, staring blankly for a moment at Madame Chalice. Then, trembling greatly, she reached to the table for a cup of water.

Madame Chalice was at once by her side. "You are ill, poor girl," she said anxiously, and put her arm around her.

Élise drew away.

"I will tell you all, madame, all; and you must believe it, for, as God is my judge, it is the truth."

Then she told the whole story, exactly as it happened, save mention of the kisses that Valmond had given her. Her eyes now and again filled with tears, and she tried, in her poor untutored way, to set him right; she spoke for him altogether, not for herself; and her listener saw that the bond which held the girl to the man might be proclaimed in the streets, with no dishonor.

"That's the story, and that's the truth," said Élise at last. "He's a gentleman, a great man, and I'm a poor girl, and there can be nothing between us; but I'd die for him."

She no longer resented Madame Chalice's solicitude: she was passive, and showed that she wished to be alone.

"You think there's going to be great trouble?"

she asked, as Madame Chalice made ready to
go.

"I fear so, but we will do all we can to prevent it."

She walked slowly toward the Manor in the
declining sunlight, and Élise turned heavily to
her work again.

There came to the girl's ears the sound of a
dog-churn in the yard outside, and the dull roll
and beat seemed to keep time to the aching pulses
in her head, in all her body. One thought kept
circling through her brain : there was, as she had
felt, trouble coming for Valmond. She felt, too,
that it was very near. Her one definite idea
was that she should be able to go to him when
that trouble came ; that she should not fail him
at his great need. Yet these pains in her body,
this alternate exaltation and depression, this pitiful
weakness ! She must conquer it. She remembered the hours spent at his bedside ; the
moments when he was all hers—by virtue of his
danger, and her own unwavering care of him. She
recalled the dark moment, when Death, intrusive,
imminent, lurked at the tent door, and when in
its shadow she emptied out her soul in that one
kiss of fealty and farewell.

That kiss—there came to her again, suddenly,
Madame Dégardy's cry of warning, "Don't get
his breath, idiot. It's death !"

Death ! So that was it : the black fever was in
her veins ! That kiss had sealed her own doom.

She knew it now.   He had given her life by giving her love.   Well, he should give her death too— her lord of life and death.   She was of the chosen few who could drink the cup of light, and the cup of darkness, with equally regnant soul.

But it might lay her low in the very hour of Valmond's trouble.   She must conquer it—how ? To whom could she turn for succor ?   There was but one—yet she could not seek Madame Dégardy, for the old woman would drive her to her bed, and keep her there.   There was but this to do : to possess herself of those wonderful herbs which had been given her Napoleon in his hour of peril.

Dragging herself wearily to the little hut by the river, she knocked, and waited.   All was still, and opening the door, she entered.   She caught up a candle, lighted it, and then began her search.   Under an old pan, on a shelf, she found both herbs and powder.   Snatching a handful of the herbs, she kissed them with joyful heart. Saved—she was saved !   Ah, thank the Blessed Virgin !   She would thank her forever !

A horrible sinking sensation seized her.   Turn-ing in pain and dismay, she saw the face of Parpon at the window.   With a blind instinct for protec-tion, she staggered towards the door, and fell, her fingers still clasping the precious medicants.

As Parpon hastily entered, Madame Dégardy hobbled out of the shadow of the trees, and fur-tively watched the hut.   When the light appeared, she crept to the door, and opened it stealthily upon the intruders of her home.

Parpon was kneeling by the unconscious girl, lifting up her head, and looking at her in horrified distress.

With a shrill cry she came forward and dropped on her knees at the other side of Élise.   Her hand, fumbling anxiously over the girl's breast, met the hard and warty palm of the dwarf.   She stopped suddenly, raised the sputtering candle, and peered into his eyes with a vague, wavering intensity. For minutes they knelt there, the silence clothing them about, the body of the girl between them. A lost memory was feeling blindly its way home again.   By and by, out of an infinite past, something struggled to the old woman's eyes, and Parpon's heart almost burst in his anxiety.   At length her look steadied.   Memory, recognition, showed in her face.

With a wild cry her gaunt arms stretched across, and caught the great head to her breast.

"Where have you been so long, my son, my son?" she said.

CHAPTER XV

VALMOND'S strength came back quickly, but something had given his mind a new color. He felt, by a strange telegraphy of fate, that he had been spared death by fever, to meet an end more in keeping with the strange adventure which now was coming to a crisis. The next day he was going back to Dalgrothe Mountain, the day after that there should be a final review, and the succeeding day, the march to the sea would begin. There could be no more delay. A move must be made. He had so lost himself in the dream, that it had become real, and he himself was the splendid adventurer, the maker of empires. True, he had but a small band of ill-armed men, but better arms could be got, and by the time they reached the sea—who could tell !

As he sat alone in the quiet dusk of his room at the Louis Quinze, waiting for Parpon, there came a tap at his door. It opened, the garçon mumbled something, and Madame Chalice entered unattended.

Her look had no particular sympathy, but there was a sort of friendliness in the rich color of her face, in the brightness of her eyes.

"The avocat was to have accompanied me,"

she said; "but at the last I thought it better to come without him, because——"

She paused. "Yes, madame—because?" he asked, offering her a chair. He was dressed in simple black, as on that first day when he called at the Manor, and it set off the ivory paleness of his complexion, making his face delicate yet strong.

She looked round the room, almost casually, before she went on.

"Because what I have to say were better said to you alone—much better."

"I am sure you are right," he answered, as though he trusted her judgment utterly; and truly there was always something boy-like in his attitude towards her. The compliment was unstudied and pleasant, but she steeled herself for her task. She knew instinctively that she had influence with him, and she meant to use it to its utmost limit.

"I am glad, we are all glad, you are better," she said cordially; then added: "How do your affairs come on? What are your plans?"

Valmond forgot that she was his inquisitor: he only saw her as his ally, his friend. So he spoke to her, as he had done at the Manor, with a sort of eloquence of his great theme. He had changed greatly. The rhetorical, the bizarre, had left his speech. There was no more grandiloquence than might be expected of a soldier who saw things in the bright flashes of the battle-field—sharp pinges of color, the dyes well soaked in. He had the gift of telling a story : some peculiar *timbre* in the voice, some direct dramatic touch. She listened quietly, impressed and curious. The impossibilities seemed for a moment to vanish in the big dream, and she herself was a dreamer, a born adventurer among the wonders of life. If she had been a man she should have been an explorer or a soldier.

But her mind speedily reasserted itself, and she gathered herself together for the unpleasant task that lay before her.

She looked him steadily in the eyes. " I have come to tell you that you must give up this dream," she said slowly. " It can come to nothing but ill ; and in the mishap you may be hurt past repair."

" I shall never give up—this dream," he said, surprised but firm, almost dominant.

" Think of these poor folk who surround you, who follow you. Would you see harm come to them ?"

" As soldiers, they will fight for a cause."

"What is—the cause ? " she asked meaningly.

" France," was the quiet reply.

" Not so—*you*, monsieur ! "

" You called me *sire* once," he said tentatively.

"I called my maid a fool yesterday, under some fleeting influence ; one has moods," she answered.

" If you would call me simpleton to-morrow, we

might strike a balance and find—what should we find ? "

" An adventurer, I fear," she remarked.

He was not at a loss. "An adventurer truly," he said. "It is a very long way to France, and there is much to do."

She could scarcely reconcile this acute, self-contained man with the enthusiast and comedian, she had seen in the Curé's garden.

" Monsieur Valmond," she said, " I neither suspect nor accuse ; I only feel. There is something terribly uncertain in this cause of yours, in your claims. You have no right to waste lives."

" To waste lives ? " he asked curiously.

" Yes. The Government is to proceed against you."

" Ah, yes," he answered, " Monsieur De la Rivière has seen to that ; but he must pay for his interference."

" That is beside the point. If a force comes against you—what then ? "

" Then I will act as becomes a Napoleon," he answered rather grandly.

So, there was a touch of the bombastic in his manner even yet ! She laughed a little ironically. Then all at once her thoughts reverted to Élise, and some latent cruelty in her awoke. Though she believed the girl, she would accuse the man, the more so because she suddenly became aware that his eyes were fixed on herself in ardent admiration.

"You might not have a convenient window," she said with deliberate consuming malevolence.

His glance never wavered, though he understood instantly what she meant. So, she had discovered that ! He flushed.

"Madame," he said, "I hope that I am a gentleman at heart !"

The whole scene came back on him, and a moisture sprang to his eyes.

"She is innocent," he said—"upon my sacred honor ! Yes, yes, I know that the evidence is all against me, but I speak the absolute truth. You saw—that night, did you ?"

She nodded.

"Ah, it is a pity—a pity. But, madame, as you are a true woman, believe what I say ; for, I repeat, it is the truth."

Then, with admirable reticence, even great delicacy, he told the story as Élise had told it, and as convincingly.

"I believe you, monsieur," she said frankly, when he had done, and stretched out her hand to him with a sudden impulse of regard. "Now, follow that unselfishness by another."

He looked inquiringly at her.

"Give up your adventure," she added eagerly.

"Never," was his instant reply, "never !"

"I beg of you, I appeal to you—my friend," she urged, possessed of the ardor of the counsel who pleads a bad case. "I do not impeach you or your claims, but I ask that you leave this vil-

lage as you found it, these happy people undis-
turbed in their homes. Ah, go! Go now, and
you will be a name to them, remembered always
with admiration.   You have been courageous,
you have been liked, you have been inspiring—
ah, yes, I admit it, even to me!—inspiring. The
spirit of adventure in you, your hopes, your plans
to do great things, roused me. It was that made
me your friend more than aught else.   Truly
and frankly, I do not think that I am convinced
of anything save that you are no coward, and
that you love a cause. Let it go at that—you
must, you must. You came in the night, pri-
vately and mysteriously; go in the night, this
night, mysteriously—an inscrutable, romantic figure.   If you are all you say—and I should be
glad to think so—go where your talents will have
greater play, your claims larger recognition.
This is a small game here. Leave us as you
came. We shall be the better for it ; our poor folk
here will be the better for it. Stay, and who can
tell what may happen? I was wrong, wrong—I
see that now—to have encouraged you at all.
I repent of it. Here, as I talk to you, I feel, with
no doubt whatever, that the end of your bold
exploit is near. Can you not see that? Ah, yes,
you must, you must! Take my horses to-night,
leave here, and come back no more ; and none of
us shall feel sorry in thinking of the time when
Valmond came to Pontiac."

Variable, accusing, she had suddenly shown

him something beyond caprice, beyond accident of mood or temper. The true woman had spoken ; all outer modish garments had dropped away from her real nature, and revealed its abundant depth and sincerity. All that was roused in him at this moment, was never known ; he never could tell it. There were eternal spaces between them. She had been speaking to him just now with no personal sentiment. She was only the lover of honest things, the friend, the good comrade, obliged to flee a cause for its terrible unsoundness, yet trying to prevent wreck and ruin.

He arose and turned his head away for an instant, so moving had been her eloquence. His glance caught the picture of the Great Napoleon, and his eyes met hers again with new resolution.

"I must stay," he answered ; "I will not turn back, whatever comes. This is but child's play, but a speck beside what I mean to do. True, I came in the dark, but I will go in the light. I shall not leave them behind, these poor folk ; they shall come with me. I have money, France is waiting, the people are sick of the Bourbons, I have the great love of our cause, and——"

"But you must, you must listen to me, monsieur," she said desperately.

She came close to him, and out of the frank eagerness of her nature, laid her hand upon his arm, and looked him in the eyes with an almost tender appealing.

At that moment the door opened, and Monsieur De la Rivière was announced.

"Ah, madame," said the young Seigneur, in a tone more than a little acrid, "secrets of state, no doubt?"

"Statesmen need not commit themselves to newsmongers, monsieur," she answered, still standing very near Valmond, as though she would continue a familiar talk when the disagreeable interruption had passed. She was thoroughly fearless, clear of heart, above all littlenesses.

"I had come to warn Monsieur Valmond once again, but I find him with his ally, counsellor—and comforter," he retorted with perilous suggestion.

Time would move on, and Madame Chalice might forget that wild remark, but she never would forgive it, and she never wished to do so. The insolent, petty, provincial Seigneur!

"Monsieur De la Rivière," she returned with icy dignity, "you cannot live long enough to atone for that impertinence."

"I beg your pardon, madame," he returned earnestly, awed by the look in her face, for she was thoroughly aroused. "I came to stop a filibustering expedition, to save the credit of the place where I was born, where my people have lived for generations."

She made a quick, deprecatory gesture. "You saw me enter here," she said, "and you thought to discover treason of some kind—Heaven knows

what a mind like yours may imagine! You find
me giving better counsel to Monsieur Valmond
than you could ever hope to give—out of a better
heart and from a better understanding. You have
been worse than intrusive; you have been rash
and stupid. You call his Excellency filibuster and
impostor. I assure you it is my fondest hope
that Prince Valmond Napoleon, will ever count
me among his friends, in spite of all his enemies."

She turned her shoulder on him, and took Valmond's hand with a pronounced obeisance, saying,
"Adieu, sire" (she was never sorry she had said
it), and passed from the room. Valmond was
about to follow her.

"Thank you, no, I will go to my carriage
alone," she said, and he did not insist.

When she had gone he stood holding the door
open, and looking at De la Rivière. He was very
pale; there was a menacing fire in his eyes. The
young Seigneur was ready for battle also.

"I am occupied, monsieur," said Valmond,
meaningly.

"I have come to warn you——"

"The old song; I am occupied, monsieur."

"Charlatan!" said De la Rivière, and took a
step angrily towards him, for he was losing command of himself.

At that moment Parpon, who had been lurking
outside in the hall for a half hour or more,
stepped into the room, came between the two,

and looked up with a mocking leer at the young
Seigneur.

"You have twenty-four hours to leave Pontiac."
cried De la Rivière, as he left the room.

"My watch keeps different time, monsieur,"
said Valmond, coolly, and closed the door.

CHAPTER XVI

FROM the depths where Élise was cast, it was not for her to see that her disaster had brought light to others ; that out of the pitiful confusion of her life had come order and joy. A half-mad woman, without memory, knew again whence she came and whither she was going ; and, bewildered and happy, with a hungering tenderness, moved her hand over the head of her poor dwarf, as though she would know if he were truly her own son. A new spirit also had come into Parpon's eyes, gentler, less weird, less distant. With the advent of their joy a great yearning came to them to save Élise. They hung over her bed, watchful, solicitous.

It must go hard with her, and twenty-four hours would see the end, or a fresh beginning. She had fought back the fever too long, her brain and emotions had been strung to a fatal pitch, and the disease, like a hurricane, carried her on for hours. Her own mother sat in a corner, stricken and numb. At last she fell asleep in her chair, but Parpon and his mother slept not at all. Now and again the dwarf went to the door and looked out at the night—still, and full of the wonder of growth and rest.

Far up on Dalgrothe Mountain, a soft brazen
light lay like a shield against the sky, a mystical, hovering thing.   He knew it to be the
reflection of the camp-fires in the valley, where
Lagroin and his men were sleeping.   There came
out of the general stillness a long, low murmur, as
though nature were crooning : the untiring rustle
of the river, the water that rolled on and never
came back again.   Where did they all go—those
thousands of rivers forever pouring on, lazily
or wildly ? What motive ? What purpose ? Just
to empty themselves into the greater waters, there
to be lost ?   Was it enough to travel on so inevitably to the end, and be swallowed up ?

And these millions of lives hurrying along ?
Was it worth while living, only to grow older and
older, and coming sooner or later to the Home-
stead of the Ages, enter a door that opened only
inward, and be swallowed up in the twilight ?
Why arrest the travelling, however swift it be ?
Sooner or later it must come—with dusk the end
of it.

The dwarf heard the moaning of the stricken
girl, her cry of " Valmond ! Valmond ! " the sobs
that followed, the woe of her self-abnegation, even
in delirium.

For one's self it mattered little, maybe, the attitude of the mind, whether it would arrest or be
glad of the terrific travel ; but for another human
being, who might judge ? Who might guess what
was best for another, what was most merciful,

13

most good ?   Destiny meant us to prove our case
against it, as long and as well as we might ; to
establish our right to be here as long as we could,
so discovering the world day by day, and ourselves to the world, and ourselves to ourselves.
To live it out, resisting the power that destroys, to
the end—that was the divine secret.

" Valmond ! Valmond ! oh Valmond ! "

The voice wailed out the words again and again.

Through the sounds there came another inner
voice, that resolved all the crude, primitive
thoughts here defined ; vague, elusive, in Parpon's own brain.

The girl's life should be saved at any cost, even
if to save it meant the awful and certain alterna-
tive doom his mother had whispered to him over
the bed an hour before.

He turned and went into the house.   The old
woman bent above Élise, watching intently, her
eyes straining, her lips anxiously compressed.

" My son," she said, " she will die in an hour if
I don't give her more.   If I do, she may die at
once.   If she gets well, she will be——"   She
made a motion to her eyes.

" Blind, mother, blind ? " he whispered, and he
looked round the room.   How good was the sight
of the eyes !

" Perhaps she would rather die," said the old
woman.   " She is unhappy."   She was thinking
of her own far, bitter past, remembered now after
so many years.   " Misery and blindness too—ah !

What right have I to make her blind? It's a great risk, Parpon, my dear son."

"I must, I must, for your sake. Valmond! Valmond! oh Valmond!" cried Élise again out of her delirium. The stricken girl had answered for Parpon. She had decided for herself. Life! that was all she prayed for: for another's sake, not her own.

Her mother slept on in the corner of the room, unconscious of the terrible verdict hanging in the balance.

Madame Dégardy emptied into a cup of liquor, the strange brown powder, mixed it, and held it to the girl's lips, pouring it slowly down.

Once, twice, during the next hour a low, anguished voice filled the room; but just as dawn came, Parpon stooped, and tenderly wiped a soft moisture from the face lying so quiet and peaceful now, against the pillow.

"She breathes easy, poor pretty bird!" said the old woman, gently.

"She'll never see again?" asked Parpon, mournfully.

"Never a thing while she lives," was the whispered reply.

"But she has her life," said the dwarf; "she wished it so."

"What's the good?" The old woman had divined why Élise had wanted to live.

The dwarf did not answer. His eyes wandered about abstractedly, and fell upon the sleeping mother, unconscious of the awful peril passed, and the painful salvation come to her daughter.

The blue gray light of morning showed under the edge of the closed window-blind. Day was mingling incongruously with night in the little room.

Parpon opened the door and went out. Morn was spreading slowly over the drowsy landscape. There was no life as yet in all the horizon, no fires, no animals stirring, no early workmen, no anxious harvesters. But the birds were out, and presently here and there cattle rose up in the fields.

Then, over the foot-hills, he saw a white horse and its rider, show up against the gray dust of the road.

Élise's sorrowful cry came to him : " Valmond ! Valmond ! oh Valmond ! "

His duty to the girl was done ; she was safe ; now he must follow that figure to where the smoke of the camp-fires, came curling up by Dalgrothe Mountain. There were rumors of trouble : he must again be minister, counsellor, friend to his master.

A half hour later he was climbing the hill where he had seen the white horse and its rider. The sound of a drum came from the distance. The gloom and suspense of the night just passed went from him, and into the sunshine he sang :

> " Oh, grand to the war he goes,
>   O *gai, vive le roi !* "

Not long afterwards he entered the encampment. Around one fire, cooking their breakfasts, were Muroc the charcoalman, Duclosse the mealman, and Garotte the limeburner. They all were in good spirits.

"For my part," Muroc was saying, as Parpon nodded at them, and passed by, "I'm not satisfied."

"Don't you get enough to eat?" asked the mealman, whose idea of happiness was based upon the appreciation of a good dinner.

"But yes, and enough to drink, thanks to his Excellency, and the buttons he put on my coat." Muroc jingled some gold coins in his pocket. "It's this being clean, that's the devil! When I sold charcoal, I was black and beautiful, and no dirt showed; I polished like a pan. Now, if I touch a potato I'm filthy. Pipe-clay is hell's stuff to show you up as the Lord made you."

Garotte laughed. "Wait till you get to fighting. Powder sticks better than charcoal. For my part, I'm always clean as a whistle."

"But you're like a bit of wool, limeburner, you never sweat. Dirt don't stick to you as to me and the mealman. Duclosse there, used to look like a pie when the meal and sweat dried on him. When we reach Paris, and his Excellency gets his own, I'll take to charcoal again; I'll fill the palace cellars. That suits me better than chalk, and washing every day."

"Do you think we'll ever get to Paris?" asked the mealman, cocking his head seriously.

"That's the will of God, and the weather at sea, and what the Bourbons do," answered Muroc, grinning.

It was hard to tell how deep this adventure lay in Muroc's mind. He had a prodigious sense of humor, the best critic in the world.

"For me," said the limeburner, "I think there'll be fighting before we get to the Bourbons. There's talk that the Gover'ment's coming against us."

"Done!" said the charcoalman. "We'll see the way our great man puts their noses out of joint."

"Here's Lajeunesse," broke in the mealman, as the blacksmith came near to their fire. He was dressed in complete regimentals, made by the parish tailor.

"Is that so, Monsieur le Capitaine?" asked Muroc. "Is the Gover'ment to be fighting us? Why should it? We're only for licking the Bourbons, and who cares a sou for them, eh?"

"Not a go'-dam," said Duclosse, airing his favorite oath. "The English hate the Bourbons too."

Lajeunesse looked from one to the other, then burst into a laugh. "There's two gills of rum for every man at twelve o'clock to-day, so says his Excellency; and two buttons for the coat of every sergeant, and five for every captain. The English up there in Quebec can't do better than that, can they? And will they? No. Does a man spend money on a hell's foe, unless he means to give it

work to do ? Pish ! Is his Excellency like to hang
back because Monsieur De la Rivière says he'll
fetch the Government ?   Bah !   The bully soldiers
would come with us as they went with the Great
Napoleon at Grenoble.   Ah, that !   His Excellency
told me about that just now.   Here stood the soldiers "—he mapped out the ground with his sword
—" here stood the Great Napoleon, all alone.   He
looks straight before him.   What does he see ?
Nothing less than a hundred muskets pointing at
him.   What does he do ?   He walks up to the
soldiers, opens his coat, and   says : ' Soldiers,
comrades, is there one of you will kill your emperor ? ' Damned if there was one.   They dropped
their muskets, and took to kissing his hands.
There, my dears, that was the Great Emperor's
way, our emperor's father's little way."

   " But suppose they fired at us 'stead of at his
Excellency ? " asked the mealman.

   " Then, mealman, you'd settle your account for
lightweights sooner than you want."

   Duclosse twisted his mouth dubiously.   He
was not sure how far his enthusiasm could carry
him.   Muroc shook his shaggy head in mirth.

   " Well, 'tis true we're getting off to France,"
said the limeburner.   " We can drill as we travel,
and there's plenty of us for a start."

   " Morrow we go," said Lajeunesse.   " The
proclamation is to be out in an hour, and you're
all to be ready by ten o'clock in the morning.
His Excellency is to make a speech to us to-night ;

then the general—ah, what a fine soldier, and eighty years old !—he's to give orders and make a speech also : and I'm to be colonel "—he paused dramatically—" and you three are for captains, and you're to have five new yellow buttons to your coats, like these." He drew out some gold coins and jingled them. Every man got to his feet, and Muroc let the coffee-tin fall. " There's to be a grand review in the village this afternoon. There's breakfast for you, my dears ! "

Their exclamations were interrupted by Lajeunesse, who added : " And my Madelinette is to go to Paris, after all, and Monsieur Parpon is to see that she starts right."

Monsieur Parpon was a new title for the dwarf. But the great comedy, so well played, had justified it.

" Oh, his Excellency 'll keep his word," said the mealman. " I'd take Élise Malboir's word about a man for a million francs, was he prince or ditcher ; and she says he's the greatest man in the world. She knows."

" That reminds me," said Lajeunesse, gloomily, " Élise has the black fever."

The mealman's face seemed to petrify, his eyes stood out, the bread he had in his teeth dropped, and he stared wildly at Lajeunesse. All were occupied in watching him, and they did not see the figure of a girl approaching.

Muroc, dumbfounded, spoke first : " Élise—the black fever ! " he gasped, thoroughly awed.

"She is better, she will live," said a voice behind Lajeunesse. It was Madelinette, who had come early to the camp to cook her father's breakfast.

Without a word the mealman turned, pulled his clothes about him with a jerk, and, pale and bewildered, started away at a run down the plateau.

"He's going to the village," said the charcoalman. "He hasn't leave. That's court-martial!"

Lajeunesse shook his head knowingly. "He's never had but two ideas in his nut—meal and Élise; let him go."

The mealman was soon lost to view, unheeding the challenge that rang after him.

Lagroin had seen the fugitive from a distance, and came down, inquiring. When he was told, he swore that Duclosse should suffer divers punishments.

"A pretty kind of officer!" he cried in a fury. "Damn it, is there another man in my army would do it?"

No one answered, and because Lagroin was not a wise man, he failed to see that in time his army might be dissipated by such awkward incidents. When Valmond was told, he listened with a better understanding.

All Lajeunesse had announced came to pass. The review and march and show were goodly, after their kind, and by dint of money and wine the enthusiasm was greater than ever it had been;

for it was joined to the pathos of the expected departure. The Curé and the avocat, kept within doors ; for they had talked together, and now that the day of fate was at hand, and sons, brothers, fathers, were to go off on this far adventure, a new spirit suddenly thrust itself in, and made them sad and anxious. Monsieur De la Rivière was gloomy ; Medallion was the one comfortable, cool person in the parish. It had been his conviction that something would occur to stop the whole business at the critical moment. He was a man of impressions, and he lived in the light of them continuously. Wisdom might have been looked for from Parpon, but he had been won by Valmond from the start, and now in the great hour he was absorbed in another theme—the restoration of his mother to himself, and to herself.

At seven o'clock in the evening Valmond and Lagroin were in the streets, after they had marched their men back to camp. A crowd had gathered near the church, for his Excellency was on his way to visit the Curé.

As he passed they cheered him. He stopped to speak to them. Before he had ended, some one came crying wildly that the soldiers, the redcoats, were come. The sound of a drum rolled up the street, and presently, round a corner, came the well-ordered troops of the Government.

Instantly Lagroin wheeled to summon any stray men of his little army, but Valmond laid an arresting hand on his arm. It would have been the same in any case, for the people had scattered like sheep, and stood apart.

They were close by the church steps. Valmond mechanically saw the mealman, open-mouthed and dazed, start forward from the crowd; but, hesitating, he drew back again almost instantly, and was swallowed up in the safety of distance. He smiled at the mealman's hesitation, even while he said to himself, "This ends it—ends it!"

He said it with no great sinking of heart, with no fear. It was the solution of all; it was his only way to honor.

The soldiers were halted a little distance from the two; and the officer commanding, after a preamble, in the name of the Government formally called upon Valmond and Lagroin to surrender themselves, or suffer the perils of resistance.

"Never!" broke out Lagroin, and drawing his sword, he shouted, "*Vive Napoléon!* The Old Guard never surrenders!"

Then he made as if to rush forward on the troops.

"Fire!" called the officer.

Twenty rifles blazed out. Lagroin tottered, and fell at the feet of his master.

Raising himself he clasped Valmond's knee, and looking up, said gaspingly:

"Adieu, sire! I love you; I die for you." His head fell at his emperor's feet, though the hands still clutched the knee.

Valmond stood over his body, and drew a pistol.

"Surrender, monsieur!" said the officer, "or we fire!"

"Never! A Napoleon knows how to die!" came the ringing reply, and he raised his pistol at the officer.

"Fire!" came the sharp command.

"*Vive Napoléon!*" cried the doomed man, and fell, mortally wounded.

At that instant the Curé, with Medallion, came hurrying round the corner of the church.

"Fools! Murderers!" he said to the soldiers. "Ah, these poor children!"

Stooping, he lifted up Valmond's head, and Medallion felt Lagroin's pulseless heart.

The officer picked up Valmond's pistol. A moment afterwards he looked at the dying man in wonder, for he found that the weapon was not loaded!

CHAPTER XVII

" How long, Chemist ? "

" Two hours, perhaps."

" So long ? "

After a moment he said dreamily : " It is but a step."

The Little Chemist nodded, though he did not understand. The Curé stooped over him.

" A step, my son ? " he asked, thinking he spoke of the voyage the soul takes.

" To the Tuileries," answered Valmond, and he smiled. The Curé's brow clouded ; he wished to direct the dying man's thoughts elsewhere.

" It is but a step—anywhere," he continued, and looked towards the Little Chemist. " Thank you, dear monsieur, thank you. There is a silver night-lamp in my room; I wish it to be yours. Adieu, my friend."

The Little Chemist tried to speak, but could not. He stooped and kissed Valmond's hand, as though he thought him still a prince, and not the impostor which British rifles had declared him. To the end, the coterie would act according to the light of their own eyes.

" It is now but a step to anything," repeated Valmond.

The Curé understood him at last. "The longest journey is short by the light of the grave," he responded gently.

Presently the door opened, admitting the avocat. Valmond calmly met Monsieur Garon's pained look, and courteously whispered his name.

"Your Excellency has been basely treated," said the avocat, his lip trembling.

"On the contrary, well, dear monsieur," answered the ruined adventurer. " Destiny plays us all. Think : I die the death of a soldier, and my crusade was a soldier's vision of conquest. I have paid the price. I have——"

He did not finish the sentence, but lay lost in thought. At last he spoke in a low tone to the avocat, who quickly began writing at his dictation.

The chief clause of the record was a legacy of ten thousand francs to " my faithful minister and constant friend, Monsieur Parpon ; " another of ten thousand to Madame Joan Dégardy, " whose skill and care of me merits more than I can requite ; " twenty thousand to the Church of St. Nazaire of the parish of Pontiac ; five thousand to " the beloved Monsieur Fabre, curé of the same parish, to whose good and charitable heart I come for my last comforts ; " twenty thousand to " Mademoiselle Madelinette Lajeunesse, that she may learn singing under the best masters in Paris." To Madame Chalice he left all his personal effects, ornaments, and relics, save a certain decoration given the old sergeant, and a ring once worn by

the Emperor Napoleon. These were for a gift to
"dear Monsieur Garon, who has honored me with
his distinguished friendship ; and I pray that our
mutual love for the same cause, may give me
some title to his remembrance."

Here the avocat stopped him with a quick, pro-
testing gesture.

"Your Excellency ! your Excellency !" he said
in a shaking voice, " my heart has been with the
man, as with the cause."

Other legacies were given to Medallion, to the
family of Lagroin, of whom he still spoke as " my
beloved general who died for me ;" and ten francs
to each recruit who had come to his standard.

After a long pause, he said lingeringly : "To
Mademoiselle Élise Malboir, the memory of whose
devotion and solicitude gives me joy in my last
hour, I bequeath fifty thousand francs. In the
event of her death, this shall revert to the parish
of Pontiac, in whose graveyard I wish my body to
lie. `The balance of my estate, whatever it may
now be, or may prove to be hereafter, I leave to
Pierre Napoleon, third son of Lucien Bonaparte,
Prince of Canino, of whom I cherish a reverent
remembrance."

A few words more ended the will, and the name
of a bank in New York was given as agent. Then
there was silence in the room, and Valmond appeared to sleep.

Presently the avocat, thinking that he might
wish to be alone with the Curé, stepped quietly to

the door, and opened it upon Madame Chalice. She pressed his hand, her eyes full of tears, passed inside the room, going softly to a shadowed corner, where she sat watching the passive figure on the bed.

What were the thoughts of this man, now that his adventure was over and his end near? If he were in very truth a prince, how pitiable, how paltry! What cheap martyrdom! If an impostor, had the game been worth the candle?—Death seemed a coin of high value for this short, vanished comedy. The man alone could answer, for the truth might not be known save by the knowledge that comes with the end of all.

She looked at the Curé, where he knelt praying, and wondered how much of this tragedy the anxious priest would lay at his own door.

"It is no tragedy, dear Curé," Valmond said suddenly, as if following her thoughts.

"My son, it is all tragedy until you have shown me your heart, that I may send you forth in peace."

He had forgotten Madame Chalice's presence, and she sat very still.

"Even for our dear Lagroin," Valmond continued, "it was no tragedy. He was fighting for the cause, not for a poor fellow like me. As a soldier loves to die, he died—in the dream of his youth, sword in hand."

"You loved the cause, my son?" was the troubled question. "You were all honest?"

Valmond made as if he would rise on his elbow, in excitement, but the Curé put him gently back.

"From a child I loved it, dear Curé," was the quick reply. "Listen, and I will tell you all my story."

He composed himself, and his face took on a warm light, giving it a pathetic look of happiness.

"The very first thing I remember was sitting on the sands of the sea-shore, near some woman who put her arms round me, and drew me to her heart. I seem even to recall her face now, though I never could before—do we see things clearer when we come to die, I wonder? I never saw her again. I was brought up by my parents, who were humble peasants, on an estate near Viterbo, in Italy. I was taught in the schools, and I made friends among my schoolfellows; but that was all the happiness I had; for my parents were strict and hard with me, and showed me no love. At twelve I was taken to Rome, and there I entered the house of Prince Lucien Bonaparte, as page. I was always near the person of his highness."

He paused, at sight of a sudden pain in the Curé's face. Sighing, he continued:

"I travelled with him to France, to Austria, to England, where I learned to speak the language, and read what the English wrote about the great Napoleon. Their hatred angered me, and I began to study what French and Italian books said of him. I treasured up every scrap of knowledge I could get. I listened to all that was said in the

14

prince's palace, and I was glad when his highness let me read aloud private papers to him. From these I learned the secrets of the great family. The prince was seldom gentle with me—sometimes almost brutal, yet he would scarcely let me out of his sight. I had little intercourse then with the other servants, and less still when I was old enough to become a valet ; and a valet I was to the prince for twelve years."

The Curé's hand clasped the arm of his chair, nervously. His lips moved, but he said nothing aloud, and he glanced quickly towards Madame Chalice, who sat motionless, her face flushed, her look fixed on Valmond. So, he was the mere impostor after all—a valet ! Fate had won the toss-up ; not faith, or friendship, or any good thing.

" All these years," Valmond continued presently, his voice growing weaker, "I fed on such food as is not often within the reach of valets. I knew as much of the Bonapartes, of Napoleonic history, as the prince himself ; so much so that he often asked me of some date or fact of which he was not sure. In time, I became almost like a private secretary to him. I lived in a dream for years ; for I had poetry, novels, paintings, music, at my hand all the time, and the prince, at the end, changed greatly, was affectionate indeed, and said he would do good things for me. I became familiar with all the intrigues, the designs of the Bonapartes ; and what I did not know was told me by Prince Pierre, who was near my own age,

and who used me always more like a friend than
a servant.

"One day the prince was visited by Count
Bertrand, who was with the Emperor in his exile,
and I heard him speak of a thing unknown to
history: that Napoleon had a son, born at St.
Helena, by a countess well known in Europe.
She had landed, disguised as a sailor, from a mer-
chant ship, and lived in retirement at Longwood,
for near a year. After the Emperor died the thing
was discovered, but the governor of the island
made no report of it to the British Government,
for that would have reflected on himself; and the
returned exiles kept the matter a secret. It was
said that the child died at St. Helena. The story
remained in my mind, and I brooded on it.

"Two years ago the prince died in my arms.
When he was gone, I found that I had been left
five hundred thousand francs, a chateau, and several relics of the Bonapartes, as reward for my
services to the prince, and, as the will said, in
token of the love he had come to bear me. To
these Prince Pierre added a number of mementos.
I went to visit my parents, whom I had not seen
for many years. I found that my mother was
dead, that my father was a drunkard. Leaving
money for my father with the mayor, I sailed for
England. From England I came to New York ;
from New York to Quebec. All the time I was
restless, unhappy. I had had to work all my life,
now I had nothing to do. I had lived close to great

traditions, now there was no habit of life to keep them alive in me. I spent money freely, but it gave me no pleasure. I once was a valet to a great man, now I had the income of a gentleman, and was no gentleman. Ah, do you not shrink from me, Monsieur le Curé?"

The Curé did not reply, but made a kindly gesture, and Valmond continued :

"Sick of everything, one day I left Quebec hurriedly. Why I came here I do not know, save that I had heard it was near the mountains, was quiet, and I could be at peace. There was something in me which could not be content in the foolishness of idle life. All the time I kept thinking—thinking. If I were only a Napoleon, how I would try to do great things! Ah, my God! How I loved the Great Napoleon! What had the Bonapartes done? Nothing—nothing. Everything had slipped away from them. Not one of them was like the Emperor. His own legitimate son was dead. None of the others had the Master's blood, fire, daring in his veins. The thought grew on me, and I used to imagine myself his son. I loved his memory, all he did, all he was, better than any son could do. It had been my whole life, thinking of him and the Empire, while I brushed the prince's clothes or combed his hair. Why should such tastes be given to a valet? Some one somewhere was to blame, dear Curé.

"I really did not conceive or plan imposture. I was only playing a comedian's part in front of the

Louis Quinze, till I heard Parpon sing a verse of *'Vive Napoléon!'* Then it all rushed on me, captured me—and the rest you know."

The Curé could not trust himself to speak yet.

"I had not thought to go so far when I began. It was mostly a whim. But the idea gradually possessed me, and at last it seemed to me that I was a real Napoleon. I used to wake from the dream for a moment, and I tried to stop, but something in my blood drove me on—inevitably. You were all good to me ; you nearly all believed in me. Lagroin came—and so it has gone on till now, till now. I had a feeling what the end would be. But I should have had my dream, I should have died for the cause as no Napoleon or Bonaparte, ever died. Like a man, I would pay the penalty Fate should set. What more could I do ? If a man gives all he has, is not that enough ? . . . There is my whole story. Now I shall ask your pardon, dear Curé."

"You must ask pardon of God, my son," said the priest, his looks showing the anguish he felt.

"The Little Chemist said two hours, but I feel" —his voice got very faint—"I feel that he is mistaken."

The Curé made ready to read the office for the dying. "My son," he said, "do you truly and earnestly repent you of your sins ? "

Valmond's eyes suddenly grew misty, his breathing heavier. He scarcely seemed to comprehend.

"I have paid the price, I have loved you all— Parpon—where are you ?—Élise !"

A moment of silence, and then his voice rang out with a sort of sob. "Ah, madame," he said chokingly, "dear madame, for you I——"

Madame Chalice arose with a little cry, for she knew whom he meant, and her heart ached for him : she forgot his imposture—everything.

"Ah, dear, dear monsieur !" she said brokenly.

He knew her voice, he heard her coming ; his eyes opened wide, and he raised himself on the couch with a start. The effort loosened the bandage at his neck, and blood gushed out on his bosom.

With a convulsive motion he drew up the coverlet to his chin, to hide the red stream, and said gaspingly :

"Pardon, madame."

Then a shudder passed through him, and with a last effort to spare her the sight of his ensanguined body, he fell face downward, voiceless forever.

The very earth seemed breathing. Long waves of heat palpitated over the harvest fields, and the din of the locust drove lazily through. The far cry of the kingfisher, and the idly clacking wheels of carts rolling down from Dalgrothe Mountain, gave accent to the drowsy melody of the afternoon. The wild mustard glowed so like a golden carpet, that the destroying hand of the anxious husbandman seemed of the blundering tyranny of labor : yet Fate, the sure-reaping farmer, was this day mercilessly uprooting tares in the good meadow of life.

Whole fields were flaunting with poppies, too gay for sorrow to pass that way ; but a blind girl, led by a little child, made a lane through the red luxuriance, hurrying to the place where vanity, and valor, and the remnant of an unfulfilled manhood, lay beaten to death.   Destiny, which is stronger than human love or the soul's fidelity, had overmastered self-sacrifice and the heart of woman.   This woman had opened her eyes upon the world again, only to find it all night, all strange ; she was captive of a great darkness.

As she broke through the hedge of lilacs by the Curé's house, the crowd of awe-stricken people fell back, opening a path for her to the door.   She moved as one unconscious of the troubled life and the vibrating world about her.

The hand of the child let her into the chamber of death ; the door closed, and she stood motionless.

The Curé made as if to rise and go towards her, but Madame Chalice, sitting sorrowful and dismayed at the foot of the couch, by a motion of her hand, stopped him.

The girl paused a moment, listening.   " Monsieur," she said, leaning forward.   It was as if a soul leaned out of the casement of life, calling into the dark, and the silence which may not be comprehended by mortal man.

" Monsieur—Valmond ! "

Her trembling hands were stretched out before her yearningly. The Curé moved. She turned towards the sound with a pitiful vagueness.

" Valmond, oh Valmond ! " she cried again beseechingly.

The cloak dropped from her shoulders, and the loose robe enveloping her fell away from a bosom that throbbed with the stifling passion of a great despair.

Nothing but silence.

She moved to the wall like a little child feeling its way, ran her hand along it, and touched a crucifix. With a moan she pressed her lips to the nailed feet, and came on gropingly to the couch. She reached down towards it, but drew back as if in affright ; for a dumb, desolating fear was upon her.

But with that direful courage which is the last gift to the hopeless, she stretched forth again, and her fingers touched Valmond's cold hands. They ran up his breast, to his neck, to his face, and fondled it, as only life can fondle death, out of that pitiful hunger which never can be satisfied in this world ; and then moved with an infinite tenderness to his eyes, now blind like hers, and lingered there in the kinship of eternal loss.

A low, anguished cry broke from her :

" Valmond—my love ! my love ! " and she fell forward upon the breast of her lost Napoleon.

When the people gathered again in the little church upon the hill, Valmond and his great adventure had become almost a legend, so soon are men and events lost in the distance of death and ruin.

The Curé preached, as he had always done, with a simple, practical solicitude ; but towards the end of his brief sermon he paused, and, with a grave tenderness of voice, said :

" My children, vanity is the bane of mankind ; it destroys as many souls as self-sacrifice saves ! It is the constant temptation of the human heart. I have ever warned you against it, as I myself have prayed to be kept from its devices—alas ! at times, how futilely ! Vanity leads to imposture, and imposture to the wronging of others. But if a man repent, and yield all he has, to pay the high price of his bitter mistake, he may thereby redeem himself even in this world. If he give his life, repenting, and if the giving stays the evil he might have wrought, shall we be less merciful than God ?

" My children " (he did not mention Valmond's name), "his last act was manly ; his death was beautiful ; his sin was forgiven. Those rifle bullets that brought him down, let out all the evil in his blood.

" We have, my people, been delivered from a grave error. Forgetting—save for our souls' welfare—the misery of this vanity which led us astray. let us remember with gladness all of him that was commendable in our eyes : his kindness, eloquence. generous heart, courage, and love of Mother-

Church. He lies in our graveyard ; he is ours ;
and, being ours, let us protect his memory, as
though he had not sought us a stranger, but was of
us : of our homes, as of our love, and of our sorrow.

"And so atoning for our sins, as did he, may we
at last come to the perfect pardon, and to peace
everlasting."

Epilogue

I.

" . . . And here, dear Curé, you shall have my justification for writing you two letters in one week, though I would make the accident a habit if I were sure it would more please you than perplex you.

"Prince Pierre, son of Prince Lucien Bonaparte, arrived in New York two days ago, and yesterday morning he came to the Atlantic Bank, and asked for my husband. When he made known his business, Harry sent for me that I might speak with him.

"Dear Curé, hearts and instincts were right in Pontiac : our unhappy friend Valmond was that child of Napoleon, born at St. Helena, of whom he himself spoke at his death in your home. His mother was the Countess of Carnstadt. At the beginning of an illness which followed Napoleon's death, the child was taken from her by Prince Lucien Bonaparte, and was brought up and edu-

cated as the son of poor peasants in Italy. No one
knew of his birth save the companions in exile of
the Great Emperor. All of them, with the excep-
tion of Count Bertrand, believed, as Valmond said,
that the child had died in infancy at St. Helena.

"Prince Lucien had sworn to the mother that he
would care personally for the child, and he fulfilled
his promise by making him a page in his household, and afterwards a valet—a base redemption
of the vow.

"But, even as Valmond drew our hearts to him,
so at last he won Prince Lucien's, as he had from
the first won Prince Pierre's.

"It was not until after Vaimond's death, when re-
ceiving the residue of our poor friend's estate, that
Prince Pierre learned the truth from Count Bertrand. He immediately set sail for New York, and
next week he will secretly visit you, for love of the
dead man, and to thank you and our dear avocat,
together with all others who believed in and be-
friended his unfortunate kinsman.

"Ah, dear Curé, think of the irony of it all !—
that a man be driven, by the very truth in his
blood, to that strangest of all impostures—to im-
personate himself! He did it too well to be the
mere comedian. I felt that all the time. I shall
show his relics now with more pride than sorrow.

"Prince Pierre dines with us to-night. He looks
as if he had the Napoleonic daring—or rashness
—but I am sure he has not the good heart of our
Valmond Napoleon. . . ."

II.

The haymakers paused and leaned upon their forks, children left the strawberry vines and climbed upon the fences, as the coach from the distant city dashed down the street towards the four corners, and the welcoming hotel, with its big dormer windows and well-carved veranda. As it whirled by, the driver shouted something at a stalwart forgeron, standing at the doorway of his smithy, and he passed it on to a loitering mealman and a limeburner.

A girl came slowly over the crest of a hill. Feeling her way with a stick, she paused now and then to draw in long breaths of sweet air from the meadows, as if in the joy of Nature, she found a balm for the cruelties of Destiny.

Presently a puff of smoke shot out from the hillside where she stood, and the sound of an old cannon followed. From the Seigneury, far over, came an answering report ; and tricolors ran fluttering up on flag-staffs, at the four corners, and in the Curé's garden.

The girl stood wondering, her fine, calm face expressing the quick thoughts which had belonged to eyes once so full of hope and blithe desire. The serenity of her life—its charity, its truth, its cheerful care for others, the confidence of the young which it invited, showed in all the aspect of her. She heard the flapping of the flag in the Curé's garden, and turned her darkened eyes towards it. A look of pain crossed her face, and a hand trembled to her bosom, as if to ease a great throbbing of her heart.   These cannon shots and this shivering pennant brought back a scene at the four corners, eight years before.

Footsteps came over the hill: she knew them, and turned.

"Parpon !" she said, with a glad gesture.

Without a word he placed in her hand a bunch of violets that he carried.   She lifted them to her lips.

"What is it all?" she asked, turning again to the tricolor.

"Louis Napoleon enters the Tuileries to-day," he answered.

"Ours was the son of the Great Emperor," she said.   "Let us be going, Parpon ; we will lay these violets on his grave."   She pressed the flowers to her heart.

"France would have loved him, as did we," said the dwarf, as they moved onward.

"As do we," the blind girl answered softly.

Their figures against the setting sun took on a strange burnished radiance, so that they seemed as mystical pilgrims journeying into a golden haze, which shut them out from view beyond the hill, as the Angelus sounded from the tower of the ancient church.

THE END.

PRINTED BY JOHN WILSON AND SON
AT THE UNIVERSITY PRESS AT CAM-
BRIDGE FOR STONE AND KIMBALL,
PUBLISHERS, OF CHICAGO.
APRIL: MDCCCXCVII

www.ingramcontent.com/pod-product-compliance
Lightning Source LLC
Chambersburg PA
CBHW030128030726
47498CB00007B/2600